By Jeanne Gowen Dennis & Sheila Seifert

Illustrated by Steven Brite

Faith Kids® is an imprint of Cook Communications Ministries
Colorado Springs, Colorado 80918
Cook Communications, Paris, Ontario
Kingsway Communications, Eastbourne, England

MYSTERY AT CRESTWATER CAMP



First printing, 2002
Printed in the United States.
1 2 3 4 5 6 7 8 9 10 Printing/Year 06 05 04 03 02

Designer: Big Mouth Bass Design, Inc
Illustrator: Steven Brite

Library of Congress Cataloging-in-Publication Data

Dennis, Jeanne Gowen.
Mystery at Crestwater Camp : book two / written by Jeanne Gowen Dennis and Sheila Seifert ; illustrated by Steven Brite.
p. cm. — (Q-Crew diaries)
Summary: In journal entries, the four members of the Q-Crew describe their investigation of the practical jokes and sabotage preceding the big competition at a Christian band camp.
ISBN 0-7814-3795-4
[1. Camps--Fiction. 2. Practical jokes--Fiction. 3. Bands (Music)--Fiction. 4. Contests--Fiction. 5. Christian life--Fiction. 6. Diaries--Fiction. 7. Mystery and detective stories.] I. Seifert, Sheila. II. Brite, Steven, ill. III. Title. IV. Series.
PZ7.D42775 My 2002
[Fic]--dc21

2002004738

**For my nephews John, Teddy, Michael, Leo, Tommy, John, and Joseph**

Jeanne

**For three great pranksters: Jeshua, Nickolas, and Austin**

Sheila

# Chapter One

# Camp Means Pranks

## PJ

"Camp isn't camp without pranks." That's what Mo said. Tried to find a book on pranks at the library. Weren't any. But I'm ready. Found some on the Internet. Could hardly wait for Sunday afternoon to come.

Was going to plan my strategy on the bus. But Candace Willoby sat next to me. What is it with that girl? She sat. She talked. And talked. And talked. Two hours of being made fun of is not my idea of a good time.

My hair's too long. My hair's too short. My glasses are too thick. Have I thought about contacts? I'm too intelligent. I don't know anything. I wish she'd make up her mind. No. I wish she'd sat somewhere else!

## JAKE

I put a frog in Candace's pocket. I figured that there was no sense in waiting until we got all the way to Crestwater to have fun. She was so busy lecturing PJ that she didn't even notice until she reached into her pocket. She screamed and jumped two feet. Pastor Boyd calmed her down. I rescued the poor frog when she wasn't looking. Score one for camp pranks!

## IZZY

What is Candace Willoby's problem? She should apologize to PJ and I told her so. PJ's a great singer. That's why we made him the lead singer in the Q-Crew band. And to think that she accused PJ of planting a frog in her pocket! PJ's not the kind of guy to pull pranks. He wouldn't know a prank if it bit him on his pudgy nose. But no matter what I say or how I try to enlighten Candace, she refuses to heed my advice.

She actually had the gall to say that I couldn't keep my opinions to myself. I told her what I thought of that! Then we made a bargain. I'm going to keep my opinions to myself this week and control my temper. (Can you believe that she accused me of having a bad temper?) In return, Candace has to apologize to PJ by Friday for how rude she was on the bus ride up. I think I certainly got the better end of this bargain. I didn't even say that, though. Mum's the word.

## MO

I was so excited to go to camp that I was up all night making plans. Once I got on the youth bus, I couldn't keep my eyes open. My mom said that's what would happen. She was right. Izzy says they sang every song they knew, but I slept through it all. I didn't wake up until we got here.

## JAKE

Lou met me at the bus. I mean, I know that a big brother is supposed to look out for you, especially when he's a camp counselor, but Lou went above and beyond. He had candy, and he said camp is more fun when you use your imagination. Nice one, Lou. I'm sure "imagination" is just another word for pranks. The best news is that I got assigned to his cabin. That'll be way cool.

## PJ

Crestwater Camp! Can't believe I'm finally here. Heard so much about it. It's going to be great! Lots of tall grass. And trees. And a lake.

First prank was on me. I fell for it. Tried to take a piece of gum from a pack on my bed. Thought it was a welcome gift—like hotel mints. But it was trick gum. The package snapped my fingers, like a mousetrap on a mouse. Two guys came out laughing from behind one of the beds. Had to laugh with them.

I got a bottom bunk. Jake's above me. It's just too tempting. One of these nights I'll get him. I intend to enjoy the whole camp experience. Especially the pranks.

## MO

Wow! I forgot how pretty it is here! The scenery is spectacular! And they have potted petunias everywhere. It seems to me it would be easier to just put them in the ground.

I have five great cabin mates: Izzy, Emma, Beth, Hannah and Cynthia. Our counselor is Susan.

I went swimming in the lake first thing. Brrr, it was cold!! Three other drummers were in the water. I guess drummers are braver—or crazier—than most people. We had a great time. My lips turned blue. I had to take a hot shower to stop shivering.

## JAKE

I met the camp's new groundskeeper. His name's Elias Greer. What a name! It sounds like him though. He's kind of old and really grumpy. He's already yelled at PJ and me twice. I'm going to have to ask my brother what Mr. Greer's problem is. All the counselors have been here a few weeks already. He should know something.

I don't remember Crestwater having a groundskeeper before. And everyone here is so nice that a grouchy person like him really sticks out. I don't like people who yell at me. Like when I cross the grass instead of taking the dirt path. He even thinks keeping the flowers from getting trampled is more important than completing a touchdown pass. Why would you work at a kids' camp if you don't like kids?

I'm glad to be away from Grandma's garden. I'm tired of planting, weeding and watering. I do miss Potterfield's two favorite dogs though. If Digby and Wally were here, they'd have a great time running around and barking at the rabbits and field mice. They could run for miles. I'd be running with them. I wonder if anyone else around here likes to run.

# PJ

Crestwater Camp is really roughing it. I found a frog in my pocket. Reminded me of Candace. Don't want to think about that. I'll have to check my pockets every once in a while for critters. Wouldn't want them to get hurt. Can't imagine how he got there. I found the frog a new home next to a lovely bunch of white petunias in pots. Hopefully it'll be safe there.

Someone was throwing water balloons at people. Couldn't tell who. Jake got hit. He took off like lightning after the joker.

There are so many petunias here. I made up my own tongue twister. "PJ picked a peck of potted, purple-pink petunias." I tried to say it five times really fast. I couldn't do it. But the petunias give me an idea for a prank. Watch out, Crestwater Camp! PJ the prankster is on the loose.

# Chapter Two

# Surprise Prize

## IZZY

I saw Pastor Boyd and the bus driver leaving and felt it was my responsibility to wish them a safe drive back to Potterfield. There's something about watching your transportation leave. I mean, I want to be at camp, but when the bus drove away, I felt a lump in my throat. It's as if all my connections with my family have been cut off for a week. My stomach is churning, and I can't help but wonder what my parents are doing without me. I've never been homesick before. But then, I've never promised to control my tongue and keep my opinions to myself before, either.

## JAKE

Mo, Izzy and I came to this camp the last couple of summers. But PJ's here for the first time. I'm so glad. Now he can help me throw Mo into the lake. I can't believe that she filled up water balloons so fast. She must have a stash of them somewhere.

There are three practice cabins, and they're all clear on the other side of camp. PJ and I used a dolly to take Izzy's keyboard, Mo's drums and my guitar over to the practice cabin. We hit a rock on one side and the dolly tilted. We almost lost my guitar. PJ dropped to the ground and started laughing. He thought it was a prank. I don't get it. He didn't make a sound about the frog I put in his pocket, but a rock in the road is hilarious?

We didn't have to bring our sound equipment. We're supposed to use the camp's sound system. That's okay with me. It's less to carry.

I found out that Crestwater has another new addition and this one's great. Her name's Ginger, and she's a golden retriever. Maybe she'd like to run around the camp with me.

## MO

I was real careful where I put everything in my cabin. I don't want anyone to get suspicious about some of the things I brought, especially Izzy. I kept thinking that if someone saw my powdered drink mix and decided to make up a drink, my best prank would be ruined. I hid most of my secret things under my mattress. I hid a few under Izzy's mattress. She'll never know.

## PJ

Everything is a potential prank. I watched everyone and everything. Nothing is going to get past me. Checked in and went over the schedule. We dropped our stuff on our beds in

Cabin #15 after we put our equipment in the practice cabin. Fifteen's a good number.

Was late to the band meeting. Was worried I would miss out on a prank.

I thought that Q-Crew was an odd name. Could not believe some of the names of the other groups we'll be competing against: Notes, Divine Design, Academy Chorale, Rolling Reeds, Heavenly Harpers, O's, Jammers, Giggles, Jingle Singers.... The list goes on and on.

## IZZY

First we checked in and then the camp director, Mr. Tabb, held a meeting for all the bands that are competing. I was amazed at how many bands came. I didn't know it was such a large competition.

## PJ

After the meeting, the frog was back in my pocket. I'll have to look into frogs when I get home. Can they smell their way back to where they want to be? He must be a soft jumper. I never felt him hop in.

## IZZY

We have two one-hour practice slots each day. About twenty bands are here from all over the country. One even flew in from Hawaii. We have been advised that the practice cabins will be fully occupied at all times. Everyone seems very nice. There is a band named the Jammers that's supposed to be the one to beat. They've won all sorts of competitions and seem pretty confident in their abilities. What a challenge! This is going to be exciting.

## MO

I must be the shortest person in the band contest. The camp took a photograph of all the bands together. Someday, I want to be in the back row of a photograph. That day wasn't today. I had to be up front, as usual.

I was sitting on the ground and a guy about six feet tall stepped on my hand. He apologized and said he didn't see me—one of the hazards of being short in a tall world. The guy's name is Gerard. He's in the Jingle Singers. He went to get me some ice. He missed being in the photograph. It didn't seem to bother him. Nice guy!

My hand really hurts. I hope I can still play. The Q-Crew is counting on me.

## IZZY

I went to the Snak Shak and bought a handful of lemon drops. A group of girls passed by me and I felt someone push my elbow. All my lemon drops fell on the ground. Then I heard Candace's syrupy sweet voice ask me if everything was okay. I ground my teeth and said that I dropped my candy. She told me that I shouldn't be so clumsy in the future and went off laughing. I guess she gave me fair warning. She is going to pull out all the stops trying to get me to lose my temper. But I'm determined. She will apologize to PJ by Friday even if the rest of the Q-Crew has to hold me down to keep me from yelling at her. I don't want to tell the Q-Crew about this deal with Candace. But if I need to, I will.

## PJ

Great cabin assignments! Jake's in my cabin. Four other guys, too. Don't know all their names yet. Seemed like friendly guys. But I'll see. Had two hours of razzing on the bus. After that, anyone seems friendly. Nice to be with Lou, too.

A bell rings when it's time to get going in the morning. Someone has to pull the bell rope and make the bell ring. Never seen anything like it. Can probably hear the sound all over the campground.

After the band meeting, I played in a volleyball game. Of course, I put the frog down in a safe place—in the petunias on the cafeteria porch.

After volleyball, I experimented with weaving a basket for my mom. Would never have thought something without electronics could be so much fun. Wish I had more time. There's so much to do here.

## MO

Oh my goodness!! The top prize is unbelievable! I'm so excited! I already knew before I came that the winners would get to come to camp next year for half price. I didn't know that there was more to the prize. Incredibly more!

One A-Chord is giving a concert here on Friday night! They're my absolute favorite group in the entire world! I have all their CDs and music videos. I just have to meet them, especially Mackenzie Sutton. She's the best female drummer in all of Christian music. Whoever wins the competition gets to open for them at Friday's concert.

That alone would be more than I could ever dream of. But there's even more! Not only do the winners get to open for One A-Chord, but also One A-Chord will add that band's city to their concert tour. The band that wins will get front row tickets and backstage passes for their families.

Oh, we just have to win!!

## Chapter Three

# Mo's Hunch

### PJ

There were two possible activities to do before dinner. We were supposed to sign up for one. Signed up for both. Did them both and still was first in line for mail call. Have to get the whole camp experience.

Good thing I sent myself two letters two days ago or I wouldn't have had mail today. Most kids didn't. I'll have to remember to write to myself a letter each night so I can get mail every day.

### MO

We played volleyball after getting all the information for the competition. Winners got to stay on the court. Losers had to make room for the next team. My cabin played twelve games straight. Wow!

We beat everyone except the campers in the cabin where Jake's brother is the counselor. There was one ball that Hannah hit way out of the court. I had to go running for it. I tripped on a potted petunia and broke the container, but I got the ball back over the net.

Elias Greer was yelling at me for breaking the pot, so I couldn't get back in the game. Whose idea was it to put potted petunias so close to the volleyball court, anyway?

Out of the corner of my eye, I saw a huge boy with dishwater-blonde hair spike the ball right at Hannah. I recognized him as one of the players in the Jammers band. Izzy said his name was Lance.

There was nothing I could do to help Hannah but yell for her to duck. Unfortunately, Mr. Greer turned his head right at that moment, so I happened to yell right in his ear. He didn't appreciate it.

## JAKE

I was so hungry. My cabin could have easily beaten Mo's in volleyball if only our stomachs hadn't been growling. I was losing energy, and I was losing it fast. We hadn't eaten since our lunch before getting on the bus clear back in Potterfield. I was so hungry after volleyball that I could have eaten some of the petunias.

I was one happy camper when the dinner bell rang. I ate so fast that after dinner I couldn't even remember what I ate. But I felt much better. I only wish there had been time for a volleyball rematch. Someone put a frog on one of the girls' tables. Girls were screaming. Guess I'm not the only one fond of frogs.

## IZZY

As usual, the food was awful, but I didn't mention it. I certainly don't come to camp because I like the food! I understand why some boys refer to the cafeteria as the slop house, because that's what they served. Slop. But I kept my lips tightly shut. Not a word came out.

Candace was watching me. I could feel it. I heard her mention that the food was great, but I didn't rise to her challenge. I kept my peace. She's not going to make it easy on me, but I can do this, unless I find amphibians on my table like some others did. That is going too far.

Chapel was a relief after dinner—food for the soul versus food for the body. I sure didn't get anything tasty for the body. At least I got a lot for the soul. We have one chapel every morning and one every evening. The rest of the time will be filled with activities and band practice.

## PJ

Played volleyball. Made craft. Ate. Almost fell asleep in chapel. Glad I didn't. Kept my ears open. Eyes open. That's how I caught it. Heard Candace lay down a challenge to Izzy. Didn't think that she would be a prankster. She seemed too self-righteous to me. She's going to be the one to watch. No one will be able to pull one over on me. I'm ready.

Decided that chapel time would be the only time when I won't think about pranks. Was grateful that the frog found its way back to my pocket after dinner. It kept me awake during chapel. I'm missing something here. How does he get in and out of my pocket so easily?

## IZZY

The camp director has everything organized down to the last item. That's why I like coming to Crestwater Camp. We are going to be covering the fruit of the Spirit all this week from Galatians 5:22–23. I put my bookmark in that place in my Bible. If we have the Spirit of God in our lives, we'll show the fruit of the Spirit: love, joy, peace, patience, kindness, goodness, faithfulness, gentleness and self-control. Our chaplain talked about love tonight. God's love shows us what love really ought to be.

When Candace came up to me afterward, she told me that I'd better watch myself. She said she was going to make things happen. I can't tell you how badly I wanted to tell her that love includes not being mean to people who are in your youth group. I didn't though. This week, I won't say a thing.

## PJ

Sore all over. Sore in places I didn't even know I had. What a wild, crazy, wonderful, busy day!

## MO

I really enjoyed the chapel talk tonight. It so relates to what I'm going through right now. I mean, I can't help it! Love is my favorite fruit of the Spirit! I love everybody, especially my family and One A-Chord. My family already knows it. And this week I'll get to tell One A-Chord! I know from their fan club website that they're supposed to be on vacation this week. What better place to vacation than at Crestwater Camp? I'm sure they're here somewhere. And if they are, they can't hide from me. Of course, once they know how much I love them, they won't want to hide.

Jake thinks that I have a stash of water balloons. I didn't tell him that I brought only three with me. That's all I could hold. But I do have a few other things he doesn't know about.

# Chapter Four

# PJ the Prankster

There wasn't much to do today. First day of camp is usually like that. I kept putting the same frog in PJ's pocket, but I didn't get much of a rise out of him. I'll try something else on him tomorrow.

Lou says Mr. Greer is a nice guy. I wonder if he's talking about a different Mr. Greer. Mr. Greer's cabin is not far from the practice cabin. I saw him planting petunias all around it. I guess he likes gardening. It figures. We're complete opposites.

I've met almost all the guitar players. The one from the Jammers is in our cabin. His name is Braden.

## MO

I love it when we break into small groups after chapel.

They call it cabin time. Susan told us that because God loved us first, he can help us love others. She said that love is a choice. We can choose to love others. I never really thought about it that way before. That's definitely something to think about.

## PJ

Played a game in the cabin after chapel. Lou was in charge. It's supposed to build trust. Kevin went first. He folded his hands across his chest. And he fell straight forward. We had to catch him. Then Tim, Ryan, Braden and Jake did it. My turn. I shut my eyes. Expected to hit the ground. I didn't. They caught me.

I must have looked surprised. That's what Braden said. I was. I never expected to be caught. I hear his band, the Jammers, is a really good band. He's okay.

## IZZY

We had our first practice tonight after cabin time. It wasn't a full practice, of course. Each band had enough time on the outdoor stage to play one song. We were just testing out the sound system. It was fun being heard by other musicians.

We played, "Holy, Holy, Holy." It's not a song we will use in the competition, but we all know it without our music sheets because we wrote it ourselves. It's an easy one to do when we're testing out the sound system and loosening up. Besides, it reminds us that we play to honor God.

The lead singer from the Jammers—I think his name is Lance—was there, and so were about ten others. I don't know the others yet, but I've been studying Lance's band. He looked really relaxed when we started practicing. But by the time we were done, I think he was trying to hide a scowl. I guess he thinks that we're going to give his band some competition.

Of course that's only my opinion, and I wouldn't dream of actually saying anything like that out loud. See, Candace? I know how to keep my opinions to myself.

## JAKE

Lou heard the Q-Crew practice. He hasn't heard us in about a year, not since he left for college. He said we sounded great. He's not the kind of person who would say that just because he wanted to make me feel good.

Lou and I had to laugh at PJ. He thinks everything is a prank. A girl dropped her tray at dinner. PJ laughed. He said it was a good one. Someone fell into the stream that separates the girls' and boys' cabins. PJ was rolling on the ground with laughter. At the practice, Academy Chorale dropped their cymbals. PJ was sure that someone had pulled one on them.

He laughed so hard that he made Lou and me crack up. People kept asking what was so funny. All I could do was point to PJ. No wonder he's my best friend. He always makes me laugh.

## MO

I asked Susan about One A-Chord. She said she doesn't really follow the music groups. But she's sure she'll like the band once she finally hears them. I couldn't believe it! I mean, everyone loves One A-Chord! Susan must be covering up what she knows about where they're hiding.

So many pranks today. So much to do. What a great experience!

Lou is a great counselor! Told him stuff. Like how I get teased. Or how other kids bully me. Suppose I was a little afraid I would be treated like that at camp. Lou said I wouldn't find any of that here. He said he'd make sure of it.

Glad we have Lou. If you stink, you take a shower. That's his only rule.

## Chapter Five

# Crazy, Mixed-up Pranks

### MO

Monday morning!! The first full day of camp! Beth is a runner too, just like Jake and I! Her group came all the way from Hawaii, and she loves One A-Chord. We ran around the entire camp this morning. There are all sorts of cabins in all sorts of little groves and meadows. Even as we ran by the different cabins, I watched to see if I could spot anyone from One A-Chord peeking out a window. I had to look carefully. I think they must be in their twenties, maybe even younger. Wearing no makeup and regular clothes, they could easily pass for counselors.

What a great disguise that would be! I'll keep an eye out

for anyone who looks like a counselor but doesn't seem to have any responsibilities.

## JAKE

Now I know camp has really begun. Last night after dark when I crawled into my bunk, everything felt gritty. It felt like someone put sand in my sleeping bag. I had to turn on the lights to see what was going on. Turned out to be salt. But it got worse. I started brushing out the salt, and flour started flying everywhere! White powder all over the place. The other guys in the cabin weren't too happy about that. Then it turned out that two other bunks had the same problem. It'll take us all week to get the flour cleaned up.

Lou just laughed. I have an idea on how to get back at whoever did this. PJ wants in on it. First, we'll find the culprit. Then we'll need a lot of popcorn.

## IZZY

Personally, I believe that I showed great self-control when I didn't mention to anyone that the beds were lumpy. With Emma in our cabin, I didn't even make a face when I felt how uncomfortable the mattress was. Emma is in our youth group and is good friends with Candace. Not that that makes any difference. I'm thankful that Candace wasn't assigned to my cabin.

## PJ

No one noticed my first prank. Put pink and purple petunias on all the boys' tables in the cafeteria. Took me an hour.

The girls moved them to their tables. Thought they were decorations. They just didn't get it. Wait till my next prank.

Mo and Izzy are acting funny. They stop talking whenever I'm around. Don't know what to think about it. Are they setting me up for a prank?

Found a harmless little snake in my pocket this morning. I hope he didn't eat the frog. I freed him down by the lake.

## MO

Joy! Joy! Joy! That's what our morning chapel was about today. I think that's my favorite fruit of the Spirit. How did the speaker know that joy is what I'm feeling? It's because at any moment I could meet a member of One A-Chord!!

Of course, the speaker told us that God's joy is more than the thrill of whatever good things are happening. It's a deep happiness and excitement from having Jesus as your best friend. We can have God's joy even when things are bad. I'll have to think about that.

Right now it's not a problem though. Everything's great! And I have joy, joy joy!!

## IZZY

We had the first practice slot after morning chapel. My keyboard and Mo's drums were turned upside down. There weren't any petunia pots around, so I know this wasn't one of PJ's pranks. He thinks we don't know that he put the petunias on the tables. He doesn't quite have this prank stuff down yet.

I don't think turning our instruments upside down was a

prank. It was lack of respect for other people's things. Whoever did this should know better. Instruments are valuable and should be treated with care. I sweetly suggested that someone in the group should report this to the office. No one seemed too keen on the idea. But I didn't insist because I'm in control of my tongue.

## MO

During practice today we were playing one of our favorite songs. When I turned the page, I was suddenly in the middle of another song. Jake was playing a third song and PJ looked totally confused. His page was upside down. Izzy was playing from memory and had her eyes closed. She didn't stop playing until we shouted for her to stop. We all burst out laughing. It was pretty funny. There was no harm done.

I wondered why our music was starting to sound a little weird. Someone had a great idea. Haven't laughed so much in days.

## JAKE

Prank #2 went off without a hitch until I realized that I had also played it on myself. Guess it was a good cover. I wonder who turned the instruments over though.

## PJ

Why didn't I think of mixing up the music? Great gag. Between practice and lunch, I signed up for rock climbing, archery and beadwork.

## IZZY

Since we're competing, I'm not going to go on all the hikes and activities that I usually do. We need to focus. I certainly won't mind. I think the others ought to focus too, but I'll let them conclude that for themselves. I don't want Candace to think that I'm imposing my ideas on my friends.

Instead of trying to influence others, I'm going to listen to other bands today. Like my parents always tell me, it's good to know your competition.

## JAKE

I think I know who pulled the prank in our cabin. It's payback time. PJ's really excited. He said something about petunias, but I'm not sure what he meant. I told him, "Forget petunias. Think popcorn."

## Chapter Six

# An Enemy Strikes

### JAKE

At lunch PJ was driving me crazy. He kept asking if it was time yet. Like no one is going to get suspicious with him whispering in my ear every ten minutes. I'm not telling him who the suspect is until tonight. Otherwise, it would be broadcast all over the loudspeakers within the hour.

### MO

Beth and I were both slurping the raspberry gelatin at lunch. I knew I liked her! She agrees with me that raspberry gelatin is best when you slurp it.

That isn't all we have in common! We both have two brothers, we absolutely love the band One A-Chord, and we're members of their fan club. Beth reminded me that One

A-Chord's supposed to be on vacation this week "in a beautiful natural setting." That only confirmed my suspicions. If this camp is not a beautiful natural setting, then I don't know what is. And One A-Chord is performing here on Friday night. So they must be here! It's nice that Beth came to the same conclusion.

I told Beth all about the Q-Crew and how we solved a mystery about our clubhouse at Potterfield Pond. She got all excited and begged me to get the rest of the group to help figure out where the One A-Chord members are hiding.

## IZZY

The only part of the baked bean and hot dog lunch that I could really digest was the announcement a counselor gave at the end of it. Does God really expect us to feel joy after a meal like this?

I can tell Candace is planning something. She just sat and stared at me during lunch. I don't like being stared at, but it won't work. I won't lose my temper.

## MO

Right after lunch I tried to get the Q-Crew to help. Jake found out from his brother that One A-Chord is supposed to get into camp on Friday afternoon. They'll set up just before their concert. I told him that that's only what they want us to think.

I tried to get Izzy to side with me. But she wouldn't say a word about it! Usually, she's the first one to give her opinion. But not today. What has gotten into her?

Well, if the Q-Crew won't solve this mystery with me, I'll

do it without them. I'm going to find One A-Chord. They can't hide from Detective Mo and her trusty sidekick, Beth.

## PJ

Came back from lunch and found a section of a cut guitar string duct taped to the outside of our cabin. A note said, "Give up and go home." I've never seen Jake so mad. He went storming out of here. Said he needed to check his guitar.

Elias Greer brought him back. Held him by the scruff of the neck like he was Digby. Jake wasn't supposed to be at the practice cabin right then. Mr. Greer wouldn't listen to us. Lou had a talk with Jake. Not sure if it was brother to brother or counselor to camper. Either way, I don't think it helped much.

## JAKE

A prank is one thing, but destroying property is something else. I can't believe that someone would cut my guitar string.

Elias Greer is making camp miserable for me. He wouldn't even let me tell him what happened. He said that rules are rules, and we have to obey them. Where is justice?

## IZZY

No one thought of the obvious. I reported the cut guitar string to the office. The vandalism and the note surprised Mr. Tabb. Only after I had handed over the note did I realize that I should have copied it and tried to match the handwriting. That worked so well in our last mystery.

Actually, now that I think about it, it didn't work well at

all. It was a fluke that we found a match. I guess it's just as well that I turned the note in. Maybe they'll dust it for fingerprints or something.

## MO

This afternoon everyone in my cabin went swimming. At least I think we all did. I know I did.

I didn't waste any time though. I asked the lifeguards and counselors who were watching the swimmers about what they knew about One A-Chord. I was even able to corner Elias Greer when he passed by the lake with a wheelbarrow full of potted petunias.

All the counselors were friendly, but Mr. Greer didn't seem too happy to talk with me. I asked him all sorts of questions about One A-Chord. He barely gave me one-word responses, and sometimes the responses were weird. I asked him which One A-Chord member he liked best. He answered, "Yes," and walked away. What was that supposed to mean?

## JAKE

I looked my guitar over carefully. Tried to find clues there. Whoever cut the wire also nicked my guitar. It still sounds okay, but somebody's going to have to pay for this. When I find the sneaks who did it, they're going to find out that they messed with the wrong person.

## Chapter Seven

# Checking Out the Competition

## PJ

Free time! Now I really get to do some stuff. Went horseback riding. To the craft cabin to see what was happening there. Took an easy hike around the lake. Checked out the camp sound system. Still made it to practice on time.

Only disappointment: I didn't successfully pull a single prank. Pranks take an awful lot of time. Didn't have any extra time this afternoon after my one failed attempt.

## MO

I covered the entire camp during free time, walking around aimlessly. At least that's how I wanted it to appear. I noticed three counselors who didn't seem to have anything to do. The first one was Jake's brother, Lou. He was swinging in a hammock. Other than hanging out at the cabin at night, he doesn't seem to do much. But I know that he isn't part of One A-Chord.

I found two other counselors, a woman and a man. Both of them looked a lot different from the photographs I've seen of One A-Chord. I was certain there was no way either of those counselors could be in the band. They were too short. They were hardly bigger than I am! And the man had a beard. I know for a fact that none of the guys in One A-Chord has a beard. It would spoil their image! I mean there's a One A-Chord look, and facial hair is not part of it.

I'm not discouraged though. I'll find them yet!!

## IZZY

I can't decide whether Jake's cut guitar string was a misguided prank or a deliberate attack on our band. It's hard to see how anyone could cut a guitar string and think it was a prank.

I know that PJ's idea of a prank is a little off. I saw him trying to decorate the gutter of Mr. Tabb's office with petunias. He was at the top of the ladder with a pot when Mr. Greer caught him and began yelling.

I have other problems to worry about though. Candace is really getting annoying. At swimming, she kept diving in next to me or kicking hard as she swam past so that I would get splashed. I couldn't say anything. That would have been giving an opinion. It's so frustrating.

## PJ

Checked out the camp's sound system. Met sound man. Name's Travis. Showed me the soundboards and all the sound equipment. So cool.

Told Travis about Jake's guitar string. We tried to figure out some natural way this could have happened:

1. The string popped because of a change in atmospheric pressure from a rainstorm. But it's been dry.
2. Jake played so hard with his plastic pick that the metal finally wore out and split apart. Unlikely. And it wouldn't tape itself to our window.
3. A raccoon gnawed at the steel string. Nah. Raccoons don't write threatening notes.

No good hypothesis.

## JAKE

First I went for a run around the lake with Ginger. She's a good running dog. I had to get my mind off of my cut string. The more I thought about it, the angrier I got. After a good run I settled down to change my guitar string.

I listened to a few bands with Izzy. I heard the Jingle Singers and the Rolling Reeds. The Jingle Singers were hilarious. Izzy kept pointing out the mistakes they made on the keyboard, but listening to them put me in a better mood. They make up jingles as good as the ones on TV. They were funny but still gave God glory.

The Reeds, on the other hand, sounded like a sick freight

train. I really don't remember a thing they played. It's better that way.

## MO

It was hot inside the practice cabin. Mr. Greer brought in a fan. He's not so bad, except that he won't tell me what he knows about One A-Chord.

## IZZY

I listened to so many bands today. I'm confident we have a great shot at winning. I'm not exaggerating about our ability either. Each band seems to have a major problem.

One group is named Giggles and they live up to their name. Every time one of them makes a mistake, they all giggle nervously. Another group called themselves O's. They start singing every song with a long, wavy "Ohhhh." The Divine Design, Academy Chorale and Notes are not quite up to our caliber either. Divine Design had a missing lead singer. Academy Chorale's guitarist has allergies and kept sneezing. Notes definitely did not play the same notes at the same time. I kept wondering if they all had the same sheet music.

## MO

Exciting news! Izzy thinks we have the talent competition in the bag. We did play really well today. But I think we need to watch out that we don't get overconfident. I've seen sports teams do that and then lose badly.

My dad the salesman says you've got to keep a humble,

helpful attitude to be successful. If you get too bold, the customer isn't as likely to buy from you. My dad's motto is "Know your stuff, put the customer first and depend on God to help you bring in the sale." I don't think there are many salespeople as good as Dad.

I guess selling doesn't have a lot to do with winning a band competition, unless you're trying to make the audience like you. Somehow, though, I think Dad's motto applies here.

## PJ

It's almost time for dinner. I'm famished. Need to stop writing in this journal and find Jake. Have to ask him if it's time to pull our prank. Did I mention that some girls were screaming down by the lake today? It was only a snake. I was hoping it was a prank.

## Chapter Eight

# A Call to Action

### IZZY

As if I didn't have enough going on, Candace has started being even more rude to me at meals. She closed a door in my face. She sat in my chair in the cafeteria at dinner when I went for seconds. And I can feel her or Emma watching me wherever I go. Do you know how eerie it is to look up and have people staring at you? Sometimes I look right back at them, but they don't even blink.

I'm feeling a little caged-in. I can't even go to the bath-house without finding them there. Their staring is so annoying. This has been the longest week of my life, and it's only Monday.

### PJ

Another three letters at mail call. I'll try to send myself four tomorrow! Camp is great!

## JAKE

I was waiting inside the practice cabin for our second practice of the day. But I had to leave. I couldn't handle another minute of the way the Melody Makers don't really make melody.

When I stepped outside, Elias Greer yelled at me for walking through the garden next to the cabin. I wasn't looking. I didn't do it on purpose, and I didn't step on any flowers. But he said I was "compacting the soil" and that it would strangle the roots.

I guess I can't win with him. I said, "Yes, sir. I'm sorry."

Let's face it. The guy has it in for me. I let him have his say and kept my mouth shut. I'm glad I did. Lou walked up right afterwards. I wouldn't have wanted him to feel ashamed of me. He would have if he'd known what I was thinking.

Things weren't much better outside anyway. With three practice cabins going all the time, it was noisy!

## PJ

After dinner I was bummed. Couldn't play softball. Had to go to band practice. Kept score for the first two innings. Then had to hightail it out of there.

## MO

That was really nice of someone to put all our instruments in the closet at the back of the cabin. I guess they were trying to protect them. It took us a while to find them though. We missed the first five minutes of our practice time. Izzy looked upset, but she didn't say a word. That's not like Izzy. I guess I'm reading her wrong. Or else she's sick or something. Nothing seems to make her spout off this week.

Our instruments seem to be having adventures of their own. First they were turned upside down, and then they were stored in the closet. At Crestwater Camp, the fun never ends!

## IZZY

The closet was filthy! My keyboard was covered with dust and dirt. No one else's instrument seemed to be as dirty as mine. I wish people would leave my things alone! Candace was in the room. She had no real reason to be there but she was. I didn't say anything to anyone. I got a rag and cleaned the keyboard off the best I could. But I can tell you that dirt on my instrument makes me angry. You can mess with me. You can mess with this camp. But no one messes with my keyboard.

Candace looked so innocent. Too innocent. She's trying to get me to lose my temper. Well, I won't do it. I'll rise to the challenge. I'll play the martyr for four more days to hear her apologize to PJ, but she had better not touch my keyboard again!

I wish my mom were here. She'd know what I should do. I sure miss her.

## PJ

Jake is still upset about his guitar string. Can't blame him. Wonder who did it. We figured the person would need wire cutters. Another mystery to solve. Seems like the last one just ended. This one shouldn't take long. How many pairs of wire cutters could be at a camp? I volunteered to watch for people who leave their activities early. Mo says that would be suspicious behavior, and they could be prime suspects.

Izzy and Mo are acting normal again. Maybe it was my imagination that they were planning to pull a prank. Still need to keep alert, just in case. Kind of wish someone would play a prank on me. Then I could play a prank back.

## MO

After practice we met about trying to find the person who cut Jake's string. We decided that this was not just a prank. It's another mystery. (Goody!!) We can solve it. I know we can. After all, we have experience.

I volunteered to look for some kind of wire cutters. I will check in every cabin if I have to. And if I happen to see One A-Chord while I'm at it ... well, let's just say that would be fine with me! This is turning into a better camp experience than I had imagined, and I had imagined an awful lot!

## JAKE

We tried to figure out who would have the most to gain from messing with our equipment. It must be another band. Only three are good enough to beat us: the Heavenly Harpers, the Jingle Singers and the Jammers. We're going to keep an eye on all three bands.

Talked to Mo and Izzy about the secret. I don't think PJ suspects anything.

## Chapter Nine

# Midnight Goings-on

### JAKE

I volunteered to make popcorn for our cabin. Of course, I had to make extra for "the plan." It took me from the time the Q-Crew meeting was over until evening chapel to finish. I filled a black trash bag full of popcorn and smuggled it from the kitchen to the bushes behind our cabin. I'm sure no one saw me. I put our cabin's bowl of popcorn by Lou's bed. No one will ever know. This is going to be fun.

### PJ

We roasted marshmallows over the campfire. All the stuff I heard about camp is true. It's a blast.

Watched the sunset. Lou said, "If God takes the time to say goodnight to us in such a majestic way, the least we can do is enjoy it." Cool line. Wrote it down so I could remember it. Think Mom would like to hear it. We get great sunsets from our backyard. It faces west.

Got back to our cabin in pitch dark. Surprisingly enough, I didn't stink yet. Didn't have to take a shower. That made for an all-around good day.

## MO

I kept my eye on the Jingle Singers at the campfire tonight. First I would sit next to one, then another. Eventually I sat next to all of them. As part of my investigation, I stared deeply into their eyes to see if they looked honest. Of course I couldn't really stare straight into Gerard's eyes. He is so tall. I don't know if they're honest or not, but the Jingle Singers sure have beautiful eyes.

If they are the vandals, they have a great cover. They are so funny that I had to hold my stomach several times. It hurt, because I was laughing so hard. People who can smile and tell stories like they do couldn't have cut Jake's guitar string.

The chaplain talked about peace tonight. How did he know that peace is my favorite fruit of the Spirit?! Crestwater is a great place to feel God's peace and think about sharing it with other people.

## IZZY

At the campfire, I learned that the Heavenly Harpers found a rotten banana inside a drum. The Jingle Singers found extra notes carefully drawn on their music with a black marker.

The Rolling Reeds are complaining that the humidity is wrong for them to play at maximum skill level. I'm not so sure about that one.

I haven't talked with the Jammers personally, but their instruments don't smell like rotten fruit, and theirs weren't dirty like ours. The Jammers' lack of problems seems suspicious to me. Besides, they looked too angelic. It makes me suspect that they're up to something.

The chaplain talked about peace at the campfire tonight. It was really good. I felt God's peace as I listened. I honestly believe that the pranks and vandalism will stop. You can't help but stop doing things like that when you hear a sermon like the one we heard tonight.

## JAKE

I woke up PJ an hour before dawn. I wake up automatically about that time. That's because Grandpa gets me up so early to work in the garden. And I've shared a room with Lou enough to know he sleeps very soundly, so we had no trouble getting out of the cabin.

PJ and I pulled out the large black trash bag of popcorn. We sneaked over to Candace's cabin and taped empty trash bags across the doorway. Then we quietly filled the gap between the bags and the door with popcorn. Whoever opens the door in the morning will be showered with popcorn.

I wish we could see Candace's face with popcorn falling down all over her. I'm positive that she was the one who put flour in our bunks. That'll teach her to mess with us.

## MO

I saw two dark figures heading toward the girls' side of the camp. Beth and I hid. They almost caught us. We can't have them suspecting us about the flour in the bunks, or we'll be in for some serious payback.

One of us kept an eye out for the two dark figures while the other changed the door signs on each of the boys' cabins. It was so easy to make Cabin #15 become Cabin #23 by lifting the wooden sign off of one door and putting it on another. Now they're all mixed up.

## PJ

Told Jake that I'd meet him back at the cabin. I had some work to do. One prank per night is not enough for the master prankster. Jake and I only took about ten minutes. What I had in mind took over an hour. Can't wait to hear what people say about it.

## MO

Getting back to our cabin took a little more time. We kept seeing two sets of shadows. We hid behind trees so no one would see us. One set of shadows melted into the blackness around the boys' cabins. They were tall. The other set of shadows separated. One went to a cabin, and the other went to the chapel. The shadow by the chapel turned out to be PJ. He almost caught us. Fortunately he was concentrating so hard on what he was doing that we were able to disappear before he saw us. We got back to our cabin and back into bed before anyone missed us.

# Chapter Ten

# The Secret's Out

## PJ

Great Tuesday morning! Another day. Another chance to experience all that camp life has to offer. It's almost breakfast time. I can't wait for everyone to see the prank I pulled. Everyone's going to love it!

I went out on the front porch to breathe the fresh air. When I started to go back inside, the sign on our cabin said #23. It stopped me for a minute. At first, I thought I'd come back to the wrong cabin last night. But Jake was in the cabin too. Then I realized that someone had pulled this prank on us. Wish I'd thought of that one. Lou laughed, then told us to unmix the numbers and hang them in the right places.

## MO

It was all over camp. Candace's cabin was popcorned! And Candace was the one who first opened the door. No one could talk about anything else at breakfast. Everyone thinks the boys in Cabin #15 did it to get back at her for the flour in the bunks. I could just die laughing. If they only knew.

## IZZY

What were the boys thinking? Now they've wasted so much popcorn that we might not have enough popcorn for cabin time. I am extremely disappointed in them.

It is so hard keeping things to myself. I'm becoming grumpy. I almost wish I could go home. I feel so alone right now, and thanks to Candace I can't tell anyone. I miss my mom.

## JAKE

Miss Innocent acted like she didn't know a thing. She claimed she didn't know about the bunks. Well, at least she found out about the popcorn. She still had some in her hair.

I hope PJ keeps his mouth shut. He's my best friend, but I know he has a hard time keeping secrets. Maybe I should have asked Mo to help me instead. I'm going to have to get PJ's mind on something else. I know. I'll send him on an assignment. I'll ask him to inventory all the markers at camp so that we can find out who wrote the extra notes on the Jingle Singers' music. If we know where all the markers are, maybe we can figure out who had access to them.

## IZZY

What is it with these potted petunias? They were set up like a tic-tac-toe game outside of the chapel. Someone sure went to a lot of work.

## JAKE

This morning's chapel was about patience. I need a lot of that. It still bugs me that we don't have a single clue about who cut my guitar string.

Come to think of it, I did notice something strange. As I was leaving chapel, the Heavenly Harpers were in a huddle doing some fast whispering. I noticed them doing the same thing after the campfire last night. Seems like I should keep my eye on them.

## MO

The chapel on patience was so inspiring! I try to be really, really patient. I have to be with two little brothers. Patience is my favorite fruit of the Spirit!

## IZZY

I can't imagine what has gotten into everyone. Salt and flour in beds. Popcorn in doorways. I even saw a pair of boy's shorts on the flagpole this morning. That was totally unacceptable. We're in the midst of a serious competition. But I suppose it's good for campers to get these immature stunts out of their systems early in the week so we can get down to the task at hand. We have a big competition ahead of us.

## MO

Except for Jake's guitar string, the rotten fruit and the extra music notes, these pranks have been great! Unfortunately, some joker doesn't know the difference between a prank and vandalism. Who cut Jake's guitar string? Is it the same person who turned our instruments upside down and hid them in the closet? Izzy thinks so. And she says it wasn't just innocent fun.

But it was the weirdest thing. She whispered her thoughts to me and then kept looking around like she was afraid someone would hear her. Jake called another meeting of the Q-Crew for later.

## PJ

Beth leaked the news! Unbelievable! Candace didn't put the flour in Jake's bed. It was Mo and Beth. Guess Jake and I jumped to conclusions. Honest mistake.

Candace hasn't said a word about the popcorn. Can't ask. Wonder what happened in her cabin this morning. Wish I'd been a fly on the wall or a frog in her pocket.

I wonder where my frog friend went.

## MO

I can't imagine One A-Chord being able to go an entire week without doing some sort of practicing. I simply have to meet them, even if we have to win the competition to do it. I've decided to pay a little more attention during practices.

I heard all of our competition today. I think I know which bands will make the finals. Winning won't be easy.

# IZZY

I have been making inquiries. It seems that the only bands that haven't had trouble are the ones that don't have a chance of winning the contest—except the Jammers. I don't think they've had any problems at all. I'm going to keep an eye on them. It seems to me that they have a motive for trying to make sure that the other bands lose. They want to win. Although, if they're as good as people say, I don't know why they would have to sabotage other bands.

# PJ

Had another Q-Crew meeting. Izzy's wrong about the Jammers. They're not the ones causing the trouble. I found Braden changing a guitar string. He said that someone had cut it. He told me that all kinds of stuff had happened so they couldn't practice. Like food on the keyboard. And dirt on the drums. They didn't want to make a big deal about it. They figured it was not a very Christian thing to do to try to get other kids in trouble. Instead, Braden said they're praying for whoever it is. And keeping watch. If they find the culprits, they'll talk to them. Try to get them to change their ways.

Sounds like the Jammers really are good guys. I asked Braden about markers. He had no idea what I was talking about. He had a dried out marker that was still in his bag from last year's camp that he said I could use. But why would I want that?

# Chapter Eleven

# Glaring Greer

## IZZY

This morning I joined the nature crafts group. PJ was there for most of it. We made picture frames out of cardboard and tree bark. I couldn't believe the way that Candace pushed in front of me in line to have first pick of the supplies. She knows she has me trapped.

If I suggested that she get back in line, she'd either catch me on being opinionated or say it's my temper. How did I get myself into this mess? She's so rude, but how on earth do I tell her without saying anything?

I was glad when we all had to go outside and gather tree bark. I found a tree that was quite far away from Candace. I hid on the back side of it, so that she couldn't see me.

When we went back inside, I finished my frame before

anyone else and left in a hurry. I keep reminding myself that I only have to live this way for a week. Some people have to keep their mouths shut all the time, like kids who have bullies bothering them. I can't even imagine what they must go through every day. I wish I could give them some of my courage and strong opinions. Then maybe they could stand up for themselves, and I wouldn't be going so crazy trying to keep my opinions to myself.

## PJ

There was so much to do today. Determined to do it all. But what I wanted to do was always at the opposite end of the camp. After nature crafts, I did water crafts with Jake. We made rough sailboats and raced them. I had to leave before the class was over so I could take rock climbing. I got there late, but the counselor let me try it anyway. They train us on a moving wall. I climbed to the top and saw the zip line. I definitely have to try that next.

No one noticed my prank this morning. I thought the tic-tac-toe game out of potted petunias would really get people laughing. Oh well. I'll have to try something else tomorrow. What can I do to really surprise them?

## MO

Where does PJ get his energy? I looked around the chapel area for clues to find One A-Chord. PJ was there. I searched the cafeteria. PJ was there, too. I walked toward the lake. PJ was running toward the horse barn. He seems to be everywhere!

I talked to the sound person today. I asked what he thought about the bands in the contest. I also asked him about One A-Chord. He smiled a crooked smile that said that he wasn't going to give anything away. The nerve of him! I felt guilty for even asking. As if I wanted to know if he thought the Q-Crew had a chance to win. That's not what I meant at all! Or maybe he was trying to make me feel guilty on purpose. Then he wouldn't have to tell me what he really knew about where they're hiding. Why didn't I think of that earlier? I think he made me feel guilty just to throw me off the trail!

## JAKE

Racing our homemade boats calmed my nerves. It was too bad that PJ left before the real fun started. Braden pushed Tim into the water. Another kid was trying to help him get out, and someone pushed him in. By the end of it, we were all wet. It was a bummer having to change clothes before going to another activity. But it was worth it to have so much fun.

The Heavenly Harpers did it again. I noticed them whispering together as I went to change my clothes. What are they trying to hide? I'll have to get closer and find out what they're saying.

## IZZY

Elias Greer came storming up to me as I was returning from archery. He told me never to step in his garden again. He told me that if he had caught me in his garden he would have me sent home. I just stood there. I couldn't believe what was happening. I was mortified. I was actually speechless, and that doesn't happen very often.

When Elias went fuming off, I looked to the side and saw Candace's grin. She looked away quickly, but not before I saw the gloating look on her face. I know she had something to do with this.

How long did I stand there? I'm not sure. I had been yelled at in public for something that I did not do. This situation is unbearable. I couldn't talk, but I had to do something. I had to. Thanks to Candace, I couldn't even tell anyone else how I felt.

Then I knew. The solution was so simple. When it came to me, I almost smiled.

## JAKE

Got a letter from Grandma yesterday at mail call. She must have mailed it before I even left Potterfield. She's planning to finish the strawberries this week and start canning peas. I am so grateful not to be shelling peas right now. Grandpa will put in his second planting of bush beans. He'll miss me. I'm sorry he has to do it alone, but I'm so sick of gardening. At least being at camp gives me one week this summer when I won't have to dig in the dirt at all.

Elias Greer was digging by the practice cabin while the Heavenly Harpers were playing. He planted yellow marigolds. They look pretty with the purple, white and pink petunias he planted there already. He's making the place look a lot nicer. He even seemed calmer. Maybe gardening actually helps him. I can't imagine how. It makes me want to do something else. Anything else.

## IZZY

Mr. Greer had just finished yelling at a band that he thought played way too loudly when I went up to him. Before he could storm off and yell at someone else, I asked him in my sweetest voice to please look at my feet. He looked at me like I was crazy.

I picked up one of my shoes and showed him my sole. I have my shoes specially made. My mother says I've always had weak ankles. The bottoms of my shoes have a triangular tread that I have never seen on any other shoe. I asked Mr. Greer if the prints he found in his garden matched the treads on these soles. He shook his head and looked at me closely. I asked if perhaps he had made a mistake, because I did not trample his gardens. I like flowers too much to harm them.

Mr. Greer nodded and walked away. He didn't apologize, but I thought I saw the trace of a smile on his tanned face. I don't think he's as tough as he wants everyone to think he is.

## Chapter Twelve

# Locked Out!

**MO**

Beth and I went swimming and canoeing. Then we rode in the paddleboats. We wore big floppy hats because the counselors have been warning us about getting too much sun. We spent most of our time together planning our strategy for finding One A-Chord.

Beth asked me about the Q-Crew and how we got started. And believe it or not, I couldn't exactly remember. I know we met at church. I guess we just enjoyed being together. When we started jamming, suddenly we were a band.

The name Q-Crew sort of happened too. First we couldn't think of a name. Then one day the youth pastor called us The Crew. We liked the sound of that, so we tried to think up something to go with it. For a while we called ourselves the Quest Crew. The letters stand for Q-urious, Unstoppable, Energizing, Stupendous, Techno-Crew. Then we shortened it to Q-Crew. I guess it stuck.

## JAKE

PJ and I went swimming with about six other guys. The lake was fantastic today! The lake bottom is a little bit mucky, so we can't do some of the stuff we do in the rec center pool, like diving for pennies. Instead, we played water basketball using a couple of inner tubes for baskets. My team won.

## PJ

Today was the day. After I took a trip on the zip line, the feat was accomplished. Jake and I threw Mo into the lake. I think she secretly liked it as much as we did.

So far today, I've also done archery, horseshoes and hiking. Asked about twenty campers if I could borrow a black marker. No one had one. Candace let me use her glitter pen. I had to pretend to write something.

Really, really tired. But I'm determined to have the whole camp experience. This week could be my only chance to be here. Now I'm going to go play volleyball.

## JAKE

I was glad PJ went back to the cabin before Mr. Greer got after me for throwing Mo in. I guess he didn't see that PJ helped. I'm getting used to being yelled at. PJ's new at this camp thing, and I want it to be one of the best experiences he's ever had. He's sure going to be surprised when he finds out the secret. I can't wait.

While we were swimming, Lance, the Jammers' main guitarist and lead singer, called out from the shore. He asked if we'd seen his capo. He was asking all the campers if they'd seen it. I guess whoever is doing the vandalism took the capo so Lance would have a harder time playing.

I don't use a capo. It's a silly gadget to change musical keys if you don't know how to just play different chords with your fingers. I know all the chords. Maybe Lance is not as good as he wants us to think he is.

## MO

I wonder how Lance could possibly lose his capo. He carries it in his pocket all the time. He never seems to let it out of his sight. He does take it out and mess with it a lot, though. Maybe he was daydreaming and left it on a picnic table somewhere.

I hope it wasn't a mean prank. The Q-Crew has got to get to the bottom of this mystery. How can we have a fair competition with so many things going wrong?

Hmm. Jake mentioned that Mr. Greer seems to hate hearing the bands play. Maybe he buried Lance's capo under his petunias! I wonder what the others would say to a midnight dig in the petunia bed.

## IZZY

Candace went too far this time. Hannah showed me how to take clay from the lake to use for sculpting. The lake clay was gooey and slimy. I didn't see how we were going to be able to do anything with it. Then Hannah showed me how to squeeze the water out of it. Eventually, it was dry enough to work with. I shaped my batch into a chipmunk. Hannah sculpted a rabbit.

Then along came Candace. She laughed at us. She laughed out loud at our creations. She was awful. And Hannah and I stood there and took it. What else could I do? What could I say? I kept thinking about how much I want her to apologize to PJ. If I didn't know better, I'd think Candace is our vandal because she is just plain mean.

## PJ

Spent some time with a really nice group of kids at leather crafting class. Made me curious about the history of leather working. I'll have to do some research when I get back to the Internet. The kids I met are in a band called the Heavenly Harpers. They're all related: brothers, sisters and cousins. Obviously, their last name is Harper. I did some sly detective work. Asked them if they had any markers I could borrow for a project. They looked at me funny but didn't answer. I made a note of it.

## IZZY

I could not believe Hannah's reaction. Once Candace left, she went back to sculpting. I didn't say anything and did the same. Then, quietly, Hannah said that she was going to pray for Candace. She said Candace's attitude was such a pity. I couldn't believe my ears. She actually feels sorry for Candace!

I hope Hannah and I can be pen pals after camp. We can learn a lot from each other about art. Maybe we can even visit each other. She doesn't live that far from Potterfield.

## MO

It's a no-go on the midnight petunia garden raid. No one wants to do it. Oh well, I didn't particularly like the idea anyway. I've got other plans for tonight.

## JAKE

I think we should get serious about looking for clues. I searched all the practice cabins, inside and out. Elias Greer thought I was up to no good. Or perhaps he had something to hide. It took all my willpower to stand there and listen to him scold me. I could have told him that the Q-Crew just solved a big mystery in Potterfield. I could have said that the camp should be grateful for our help. But I didn't. Better not to let on just in case he's the one.

I don't like Elias Greer. I wish he would leave Crestwater and take his frustrations with him. At least he didn't catch me snooping until after I found out what I wanted to know. The Heavenly Harpers' big secret is that one of their members is sick at home. They gather to pray for him as often as they can.

## PJ

Travis the sound guy says that I can hang out with him while he gets things set up for the competition. This is going to be so cool. The soundboard is computerized and locked up in a cabinet. This is right up my alley. I thought I'd miss e-mail and the computer this week. But if I get to learn how to operate the sound system, I won't suffer electronic withdrawal. I checked for black markers in the sound cabinet. Only found a red one.

I'm really getting confused about Izzy and Mo. They hardly spoke to me all morning, but giggled every time they saw me. At least Ginger wants to be with me. She followed me over to the Snak Shak. We shared an ice cream cone. It's nice to be loved just for myself, even if it's by a dog.

## IZZY

These "accidents" are upsetting me. We couldn't even rehearse this afternoon. When we arrived at our practice cabin after lunch, the door was jammed shut. We pushed and shoved and tried to get in, but it wouldn't budge. Someone suggested that the weather might have made the door expand. I doubt it. My theory is that someone did not want us to practice.

All the windows that we could see were shut and locked. The window on the south side is so overgrown with trees and plants that we didn't even try to get to it, but it appeared to be closed too. By the time the camp handyman got the door open, our scheduled rehearsal time was over and the O's were there for their practice. This was no accident. Someone didn't want us to practice.

This is getting serious. Are all the problems a coincidence? I think not. There are nineteen other bands in this competition who want to win. Is someone trying to scare us away? Don't they know that we don't scare easily?

## MO

Izzy was upset about missing practice today, but I wasn't. It gave me time to search for the wire cutters…and One A-Chord.

Beth propped me up so I could peek in windows of suspicious cabins. I saw Candace blowing her nose, Lou smiling at himself in a mirror and Gerard helping Mr. Greer move a petunia from a broken pot to a new one. Someone must have broken the original pot. Just for the record, it wasn't me!

There are lots of small cabins on the grounds. Beth and I took a camp map and divided it into four sections. We're planning to check out the whole camp one section at a time. I hope One A-Chord doesn't keep changing locations to throw us off.

## JAKE

Some of us went on a hike. The counselor let me run all the way back from it. It was fun, but I was so hot and sweaty when we got back that I drank a quart of water.

I spent some time with Lou during his break. It's nice having my brother up here. I don't get to see him much now that he's in college. We stuck grass blades between our thumbs and made them whistle. Then we skipped stones on the part of the lake where no one swims. We wrestled in the grass and tossed a football. It was like old times.

Funny thing was, I saw Elias Greer watching us. He actually smiled!

Candace must have reported the popcorn incident. Lou mentioned that Candace's cabin had a big mess in it this morning. He remembered that I popped a bunch of popcorn yesterday. Lou laughed, but I guess it should be no surprise that I have to help do dishes after lunch tomorrow. PJ, too. Oh well, at least we'll get an early taste of tomorrow night's desserts.

## Chapter Thirteen

# Western Welcome

### IZZY

I decided not to go horseback riding this year. All I need is to fall off and break a finger. Or have someone sabotage my horse. I could ride off into the distance and never be heard from again. I don't do well on horses.

I did go over to the ceramics cabin after what should have been our band practice. They call it the Art Shelf. I chose a large plate that has a raised mountain scene on it. I spent over an hour painting it. Hannah joined me. She painted a mug that has a wolf on its handle. She said her father was really going to like it.

We both paid the extra dollar to have our projects glazed. Tomorrow our ceramics should be done. I painted both of my parents' names on the plate. I can't wait to give it to them.

I was able to reschedule our rehearsal for after chapel this evening. We'll miss a video, but practicing is more important.

## MO

I bought all of the red licorice from the Snak Shak, every last piece. It cost me all the spending money I brought. But I happen to know that all the members of One A-Chord absolutely love red licorice, especially their drummer, Mackenzie Sutton. I read it in a magazine. Well, at this camp, if she wants red licorice, she's going to have to come to me!

## PJ

I knew I forgot something. Sunscreen is a must for camp. Found out why. Face feels tight. Hurts. Looks like I'm blushing all the time. Candace mentioned it. Handed me a bottle of sunscreen after dinner. Strange. But I'm not complaining.

Caught Mo and Izzy laughing and pointing at me. What is up with those two?

I'm going to have to miss the western movie tonight because of band practice. I'll sing fast. Maybe I can get there in time to see the end.

## IZZY

At afternoon mail call today, Candace took my letter from the counselor and acted like she was handing it to me. She handed it to me, but she didn't let go! So my letter tore in half.

I learned something today. I am no longer getting upset with Candace's antics. She is annoying, but so very predictable.

Instead of blowing up, I merely picked up the two halves of my letter, pieced them back together and started reading it. It wasn't that big a deal. The letter was from Mom. It was so good to hear from her.

## PJ

Got three letters this afternoon. Didn't open them. Know exactly what they say. I wrote them. It's not as much fun as getting mail that you haven't sent yourself. I guess I'm not a suspect. None of my letters were written with black marker.

## MO

I was getting really discouraged about our One A-Chord investigation when Beth gave me the most amazing news. The camp told all the parents that One A-Chord would be here. They invited families to come for Friday night's concert.

Now I'm more sure than ever that One A-Chord is here at Crestwater Camp! We just have to find their exact location.

## JAKE

We had a chuck wagon dinner by the campfire. They did it like the cowboys of the Old West. We had beans, baked potatoes, barbecued beef, cornbread, coleslaw and apple crisp on tin plates. It was so much fun trying to act like cowboys. We pretended that Ginger was one of the cattle that we were trying to round up. Trouble was, she didn't understand that cattle aren't supposed to bark.

Ginger's such a good sport. Afterwards, she sat by me, and

I petted her while we sang western songs like "Get Along Little Doggie" and "Home on the Range." That's not our usual style, but it was fun to hear the band singing songs like that.

## IZZY

Our chapel tonight by the campfire was on kindness. We talked about how we stray away from God when we sin, then he has to round us up like stray cattle. God corrects us and helps us see that we were wrong. When we're sorry, he forgives us and helps us learn to do better.

The study helped me realize how kind God is to us, even when we have messed up. It was a good reminder that God wants us to be kind to others, too. Even Candace.

## MO

The fruit of the Spirit tonight was kindness. I'll be so kind to One A-Chord when I finally meet them! Kindness must be the most important fruit of all. It's my favorite. Chapels have been great!

## IZZY

We had a horrible band practice after chapel. Many of PJ's notes sounded more like squeaks. Mo's drumming was off the beat. I'm not sure what else actually happened. I just know that we sounded terrible. I didn't play my best either because I was expecting something bad to happen.

I know God doesn't want us to worry about bad things that could go wrong. We shouldn't live in fear. I'm going to have to talk to him about how these vandals are making me feel. I never feel this way at home.

## MO

My drums were filthy tonight! I felt awful when I first saw them. I was feeling guilty for neglecting them. Then I saw the flower petals on the floor near my set. Someone had spread dirt on my drums on purpose! It was fresh dirt, like potting soil. I was not happy. Right away, I suspected Elias Greer. He acted funny when I saw him earlier, as if he wanted to get away really fast. I think he had a guilty conscience. How did a man like him get hired at Crestwater?

## JAKE

Flower petals! I knew it! Greer is now definitely a suspect, our top, number one suspect. His name is real big on my list. Or it would be if I actually had a list.

## IZZY

I've thought and thought about the things that have happened to our instruments. I don't know why I tend to immediately think of Candace. I have to stop doing that. She's keeping me from picking up clues that could be valuable to the Q-Crew.

Honestly, I don't think that this is Candace's work. I know that she's mean-spirited, but she wouldn't actually ruin anything. She's mostly talk. She doesn't actually do very much. This has to be the work of a vandal.

After rehearsal, I tried to deduce how dirt got on my keyboard. The dirt was mixed with flower petals. Who would have access to petals? Actually anyone here at camp would. Those potted petunias turn up everywhere. Mo is convinced that the groundskeeper is taking out his nasty temper on our instruments. But it could easily be someone else. After all, I don't have an opinion this week. Not one. Not at all.

## PJ

Saw the last half hour of the western. It was great!

I finally pulled my prank on Jake. I stuffed the extra plastic trash bags into his sleeping bag. So, tonight when he gets in and expects to slide his feet to the end of it, they will stop halfway down. I think he'll laugh about it. At least I hope so. Even Jake is acting weird toward me now. I don't get it. Did I do something to offend the Crew? Maybe it's time for that shower.

## JAKE

Lou told me that the camp is going to start locking the practice cabins at night. I think that's a good idea. But Greer has a master key.

When I got back to our cabin, PJ was acting funny. He kept talking really fast, like he was nervous or excited or something. I found out why when I tried to get into bed. He sure has adjusted to camp life. He's becoming Mr. Pranks himself.

One more day until PJ finds out. I'm staying cool. He has no clue.

# Chapter Fourteen
# Pranks in Reverse

**MO**

I couldn't risk taking Beth with me on the prank tonight. She let out that we'd put the salt and flour in the boys' bunks. I played dumb, but everyone knows. Anyway, I brought blue, green, red and purple powdered drink mix to camp just for this prank. I didn't know how I was going to get into the boys' bathhouse, but the perfect solution came right along! I ran into PJ. He's probably trying to figure out what to do next with the potted petunias. I know he's the one who moves them around every night. Anyway, all I had to do was make up an excuse to get him to stand outside the bathhouse door. I sneaked in behind him and he never noticed. I can be really quick when I need to be, which was tonight.

I unscrewed two shower nozzles and poured powdered

drink mix into them. Then I screwed them back on. The boys won't know what hit them until they come out of the shower with dyed skin. I can't wait to see the rainbow-colored assortment of boys at breakfast tomorrow.

## IZZY

Yesterday's talks on peace didn't have much effect on the camper pranks. I hope tonight's talk on kindness will.

It was getting late when I heard a sudden scraping noise outside. I knew that another act of vandalism was being performed. I quietly slipped out of my cabin to catch the perpetrators. They were raccoons! Someone left candy out on the picnic table, and raccoons were cleaning it up. They were so large, and there were four of them. I hurried back inside. I think the raccoons must be the reason that the camp is always so clean.

## JAKE

I slipped out of the cabin without PJ. Actually, I'm not sure where he was. I told Lou I needed to get the bugs out of my legs, then I wanted to take a shower. Promised him I wouldn't stay out too late. There were a lot of people out tonight. I saw one tall shadow leave the boys' side of camp. And then another short shadow entered the boys' bathhouse. That had to be Mo. I waited until she was done and then checked the place thoroughly. It took me a while, but I found the powdered drink mix. Good one, Mo.

Good thing I caught her. I would have been the first one to turn on a shower and turn green. It didn't take long to clean out the showerheads. I only wish I could have saved the powdered drink mix somehow and put it into the girls' showers. I can't wait to see Mo's reaction when nothing happens.

## MO

I almost bumped into someone in the dark. I have never been so scared! It was Beth. She had a container of petroleum jelly that looked half empty. We both laughed really hard with our hands clasped over our mouths. We couldn't make a sound. All that silent laughter made my stomach hurt. After that, we were worn out. And we knew that if we didn't go in soon Susan would start looking for us.

## JAKE

By the time I finished my shower, the other prankster out tonight must have finished her work. I couldn't catch her. I sneaked into the cafeteria and did a little prank of my own. Then I had to get to sleep. I didn't want to miss out on any of the fun by oversleeping and missing breakfast.

My hand slipped on the knob to my cabin. Someone had petroleum jellied the doorknob. So I couldn't go to sleep yet. Mo must have been busier than I thought. I had to sneak in, get my own petroleum jelly and get to work. Lou was conked out and never knew I left again.

## PJ

I had a lot of work to do tonight. This time, I knew I had a great idea. It took me over an hour to gather all of the potted petunias I needed. I'm on a roll. Got Jake last night and will get the rest of the guys today. When I came in, Lou opened one eye, but he didn't say anything.

## IZZY

I don't think I slept a wink all night, but when morning came, everything smelled fresh and new. Surprisingly enough, I felt rested. I tried to wake Mo up. I was sure that she would want to catch the sunrise. The sky was a light gray. The sun would be up any moment. She hit my hand away. Who knows what's making her so grouchy!

I quickly got dressed and went out onto the porch. It was a gorgeous morning! It was a little chilly though. I decided to get a jacket to put over the sweatshirt I was wearing. I turned back to the door and tried to open it. My hand slipped. Someone had greased the doorknob.

With a sigh, I knew what I had to do. I was going to miss the sunrise. I went to the bathhouse, got paper towels and cleaned up all the doorknobs on the girls' side of the camp. The boys pulled this disgusting prank, but they would get no satisfaction from it.

## Chapter Fifteen

# Anger, Fear and Mr. Greer

### JAKE

I went to the boys' bathhouse early Wednesday morning and saw the petunias. Pots of them were everywhere. On the floor. In the sinks. Around the showers. It looked like a PJ prank. Only PJ could think up something that lame. Besides, I followed a petal trail from our cabin. There were even some leaves on his blanket. I got rid of the evidence for him. It gave me an idea for the final prank of camp.

### MO

What a shock! None of the boys had stains on their skin this morning. I don't believe Jake. He said that boys never take showers at camp. It takes all week before they stink enough to need one. Why would he say that to me out of the blue unless he knew what I had done? Next time I'll put the powdered drink mix in the sink faucets. They must wash their hands once in a while. And I'll make sure that Jake isn't on to me. I have a few packages left.

I decided to skip breakfast so I could question the kitchen staff. They made me eat while I was talking with them.

I looked at the list of food they're going to serve in the next few days. The One A-Chord members have lots of favorite foods listed on their website. But not one is being served this week. I think that's being a little inconsiderate. I mean, they are really important stars! I gave the kitchen staff some meal suggestions.

## PJ

Why didn't I think of it? Breakfast was unbelievable. I was laughing so hard that I almost didn't eat anything. Someone had loosened the lids of all of the pepper shakers. When I went to put pepper on my eggs, all the pepper poured out. Kids were doing it all over the cafeteria.

Then it only got better. There was sugar in the salt containers! Jake puts salt on everything he eats. I noticed that he didn't use any today. I know that he's the one behind all of this. But I won't say a word.

## JAKE

Mo looks so confused! It's driving her crazy that her prank didn't work. I haven't heard any girls complaining about the greased doorknobs yet. I don't get that.

## MO

I saw PJ taking a trail ride, and I almost wished I had time for horseback riding. But I can't plan something that takes two hours. Searching for One A-Chord is my main job right now. I just have to meet them!

## IZZY

I can't help but wonder if we are going about this all wrong, but how do you set a trap for a vandal? It's so hard to believe that one of the kids or adults around me is doing all of these terrible things. Does someone really want to ruin good instruments?

The Harpers found a rotten fish in one of their horns this morning. One of them had left something in the practice cabin and had gone to retrieve it before breakfast. She said the whole practice cabin smelled like rotten fish. I'm certain that the smell will attract unwanted animals. I wish people would think before they act. Yes, I'm grumpy. After all, I'm hungry. I had a mound of pepper all over my eggs this morning. I couldn't eat them.

## PJ

The chapel talk was on goodness. Because God is good all the time, I can know what goodness is. And God helps me be good the way he is. Deep thought. Have to think about that one some more. Would like to talk to Mom about it.

Travis let me work with him right after chapel. It was great! He reviewed everything he taught me about using his professional soundboard.

Izzy and Mo are still acting strange. In fact, I'm sure they're avoiding me. Except when absolutely necessary. I took a shower this morning. Maybe I need to floss my teeth.

## MO

Goodness is a great fruit of the Spirit! It's really hard to choose a favorite fruit of the Spirit, but I think goodness is my favorite!

## JAKE

Mr. Greer is on the rampage again. Why does he always get after me? Someone stepped in one of his flower gardens and smashed some petunias. It wasn't me. Mr. Greer was also complaining about the bands playing too loudly and practicing too late. His cabin is right in the middle of the practice cabins. He says the bands are "disturbing his nightly reading." That's not my fault. Why does he complain to me about it?

I thought this week was supposed to be for the band competition. Practicing is part of it. Why on earth didn't Mr. Greer take this week off? He doesn't have to listen to the bands. Why can't he find something to do somewhere else in the camp instead of putting in flower beds around the practice cabins? I can't wait until we prove that he's our vandal.

## MO

I looked through all the cars parked in the lot. There were a couple of buses, one very cool four-wheel drive and a bunch of beat-up heaps. The counselors are college students with no money for nice cars. I didn't see any buses or vans with the "One A-Chord" name on it. There was no limousine or license plate that would have given them away either. One A-Chord members are too good at hiding in plain sight!

## IZZY

Jake, Mo and I met at the picnic tables to discuss the PJ secret. Candace came over and sat nearby so she could hear what we were saying. We said very little about the PJ thing or the case. I couldn't even give my opinion of Mr. Greer. I now know that he is not the person we're looking for. I don't know why. Call it women's intuition. Maybe it's because of that half smile of his. On the inside, I'm sure he's a very kind man. With Candace there, though, I didn't take any chances. I didn't say a thing. I'll tell the others later.

I was proud of myself. I didn't even get upset when Candace blew the fluffy white seeds of a dandelion at me. I smiled at her. She is popular, but she doesn't ever have the same set of friends for long. I think Hannah is right. I should pray for her more.

## JAKE

Elias Greer is totally unreasonable. He yelled at me again. I'm sorry, but this is a camp, not a posh resort where everything has to stay just perfect. We're supposed to enjoy the outdoors. That means running on the grass and playing football and soccer. Can I help it if Ryan couldn't catch my pass? If Greer hadn't planted those silly flower beds all over the place, we wouldn't have to worry about where the balls land. Those flower beds are a big problem.

Besides, he's the one who's trying to sabotage our instruments and ruin the competition. He's always complaining about the noise. He doesn't like kids. He doesn't like music. He can get dirt, and he has keys to the practice cabins. It all adds up.

I've had enough of Mr. Greer's yelling. I feel like pulling up all those pesky flowers of his and tearing them to pieces.

## MO

Jake asked me to look in Mr. Greer's cabin for clues. Beth hoisted me up. I couldn't believe what I saw. He had One A-Chord posters all over. I would never have even thought that he was a fan. He always acts as if he hates music. While we were at it, we looked in two other nearby cabins. Messy. Messy. Messy. But no clues.

## IZZY

Some of the other bands sounded awful this morning. I think they are under the same fear that I was last night. I'm going to talk with some of the other keyboarders. I'm going to tell them that they need to keep their eyes on God and not on what could happen to their instruments next.

Oh, I can't. That Candace! Let's see. Without giving an opinion, what can I do? Maybe I could talk to them without giving an opinion. No, that would probably get me in trouble. But I can pray for them.

Let's see, what helped me when I found dirt marks on my

keyboard? Well, besides wanting to get after whoever did it, I needed someone to listen to me and take me seriously. That's it. That's what I'll do. I'll be available to listen to the members of other bands when they have problems. I won't tell them what has happened to me. I'll listen and try to help them through this.

I hope Jake doesn't follow through with his plan to take revenge on Mr. Greer. Maybe I should say something to Jake. It's more important to try to sway him away from something he'll regret than to keep my bargain with Candace.

## MO

Since I've never seen One A-Chord in person, I realized that I might not recognize them right away. That's why I still have so many suspects to check out. I finished investigating two more counselor suspects. One woman called herself Shanna, and I could never catch the other woman's name. The nameless woman said that she did not like red licorice when I offered her some. I ruled her out right away.

Shanna, on the other hand, thanked me for the licorice. She was about the right size for one of the One A-Chord singers. She had the right hair coloring and she likes licorice. I didn't recognize her, but when I forced my eyes to go blurry, I thought she could be mistaken for Naomi Barfield. Then her break was over and she went to the horse barn to muck out the stalls. That's what she said. "Muck" is a nice way of saying that she has to clean up after the horses. Gross!

## IZZY

The Heavenly Harpers played great today. I stood there and listened. Music can be so beautiful. I was surprised that it didn't depress me to hear another band playing so well. I mean, I want to win. I really, really want to win. But I think I've figured something out. It's not about winning. It's about playing with everything you are, with all the talent you've been given, to glorify God.

The problem was that I had to stand in the flower bed to hear them well. I tried not to put my whole weight down on the soil. I turned around just as Mr. Greer came up behind me.

Chapter Sixteen

# Frantic Antics

## IZZY

I told Mr. Greer that I was listening to the Heavenly Harpers practice. I apologized for standing in the flower bed, but I could hear the music better from that position. I pointed out that I didn't step on any plants. He looked down to verify what I said.

Then I mentioned how well the Harpers were playing. He stood there with me for a minute and listened. Then he walked away. He had that half smile on his face again. It's odd, but I'm actually starting to like Mr. Greer.

## PJ

Ran the obstacle course. Over the wall. Through the barrels. Under the bars. Up and down hills. Across the pond. Set a record. I had to. The folklore talk was about to start. I didn't want to miss it.

The speaker was really cool. Had Native American artifacts and instruments. Played them. Told stories. Wanted to hear it all, but had to leave ten minutes early. Got to the practice cabin with three minutes to spare. Too bad. I could have heard three more minutes of the folklore talk.

## MO

At first, I couldn't figure out why PJ's tambourine didn't make a sound when I pulled it out for rehearsal. Then I discovered the problem. Someone must have spent a long time putting those peanuts between the little tambourine cymbals. I started cleaning them out right away so we could start practice on time.

Who would have thought up such a crazy prank? Maybe that's why One A-Chord hasn't surfaced. They've probably seen all the pranks that have ever been done and don't want anything to happen to their instruments. I don't blame them. I'm going to have to concentrate more on this mystery. We need to solve it so that they'll feel safe. Then maybe they'll come out of hiding.

PJ ran in all out of breath. I showed him what I was doing. He groaned and started helping me. Izzy was running frantically all over the cabin.

## IZZY

I couldn't believe that we were hit again! When I was setting up for rehearsal, I couldn't find the power cord to my keyboard. At first I assumed that I had misplaced it. But I would never do that. I'm very careful about my equipment. Then I thought that someone else had borrowed it. But it wasn't with any of the other instruments. Finally I couldn't help but wonder if someone had stolen it.

I proceeded to search the entire practice cabin. I couldn't check the back storage closet because it was locked. Campers aren't supposed to use it, even though that's where we found our instruments on Monday. I looked everywhere, even in the disgustingly dusty closets at the front. Jake checked up in the rafters, thinking someone might have thrown it up there. We even checked out the other practice cabins. My power cord was nowhere to be found. I was so depressed. I sat there staring helplessly at a keyboard that could not produce even one note.

## MO

Izzy doesn't make sense sometimes. She didn't have to yell at me. My hands weren't all that greasy from the peanuts. Besides, I was only trying to help. I was sure we could rig up something to make her keyboard play. Last year in science we made electricity with an orange and a nail. Or was it a potato and a fork? Whatever it was, I was sure we could rig up something to get Izzy's keyboard working. Here I was willing to use my inventive talents, and she didn't even appreciate it!

## JAKE

When Izzy and Mo started arguing with each other, I left. We weren't going to be able to practice anyway, so I headed for the lake. That's when I found Izzy's power cord. It was right in the middle of an anthill. I brought it back to Izzy, and we practiced after all.

I don't see how someone can sabotage so many instruments without leaving a trace. This doesn't make sense unless that someone is Elias Greer.

## MO

Jake shook off the power cord before giving it to Izzy, but Izzy kept wiggling during the rehearsal like she could feel bugs everywhere. I was sure it was her imagination. I get that way sometimes when I see bugs. The way she moved was just too funny! I couldn't help laughing a little.

I felt badly afterwards. She asked me to help her look for ants, and we found three on her. Poor Izzy! What a trooper for playing on. It must have been miserable going through the whole practice with ants crawling all over her.

## IZZY

I was so relieved after our band practice today. Now I know it was my imagination that PJ's voice was changing and that Mo's drums were off beat. Our sound was right on track, even if the ants did decide to dance to the music all over my poor body.

## JAKE

I didn't go to an activity after practice. I followed Mr. Greer. He never knew I was there. As I watched him work, I noticed how pretty all the flowers looked. It made me feel ashamed for even thinking about hurting Mr. Greer by pulling his flowers up. Gardening is backbreaking, sweaty work. I know that from personal experience. No matter how grumpy he is, he doesn't deserve what I thought about doing. I had to ask God to forgive me for how disrespectful I've been in my thoughts.

After a while, I saw Mr. Greer go into our practice cabin. I was excited. I was sure I'd catch him red-handed. But he set up two guitars that had fallen over and dusted off a drum set that had dirt on it. I stopped watching him and started watching a couple of birds with their young chicks.

I was about to leave when suddenly I heard an unbelievable guitar player inside the cabin. I was afraid Mr. Greer would make him stop playing before I could see who it was.

# Chapter Seventeen

# Face to Face

## MO

After our rehearsal, I convinced Izzy to take a nature hike. We had a list of things we were supposed to observe. I was trying to observe any clues about One A-Chord. Izzy's mind was on the trouble with the instruments. She kept going on and on about what the vandals' motivations could be. I think the question is a lot easier than that. Who would have access to peanuts? Either the vandals brought peanuts with them or they bought them at the Snak Shak.

I went and asked the counselor working in the Snak Shak if anyone had recently bought peanuts. She narrowed the list down to about thirty kids but didn't know any of their names. That wasn't much help. I'll have to try a different angle.

As it turns out, a lot of other people in this camp like red licorice too. People have been asking for it, so the store special-ordered another whole case! And I don't have the money to buy it. I don't even know what I'm going to do with what I have.

Now Mackenzie Sutton can get red licorice any time she wants to from the store. Another plan is down the drain. What a bummer! I wonder if the Snak Shak takes returns.

## JAKE

I couldn't believe my eyes. When I peeked through the practice cabin window, no one was inside except Elias Greer! He was playing the guitar. Anyone who plays guitar that well and with that much feeling would not harm an instrument. I'm sure of that. He was immediately off my suspect list.

Suddenly, I heard yelling on the path. Mr. Greer must have heard it too. He put his guitar away and shot out of the cabin.

## IZZY

Is there no end to the depth to which Candace will sink? She broke my plate. She ran straight into me while I was carrying it carefully to my cabin. How could she have done it? How could she have broken the plate that I was going to give to my parents?

As I stared down at the shattered pieces, I was so angry that I was shaking. In a silvery sweet voice Candace asked if I was okay. I stared at her. Then, as she was leaving, it came to me. In a voice just as sweet, I told her that I was fine. And that I was looking forward to Friday when she would have to apologize to PJ.

You should have seen her face. I wish I had a camera. Her face turned a deep red and she began calling me all sorts of names. I knelt down and picked up what was left of my plate.

Mr. Greer came up to us and asked Candace to leave. He told her to go to her cabin until she got back in control. And then, surprise of all surprises, he knelt down and helped me pick up the shattered pieces. In a low voice he told me that I should learn to stand up for myself. I smiled. Mr. Greer is so much nicer than he lets on. I told him that some things are better left to God's care. We stood up, and he started to turn away from me. I'm sure I saw that trace of a smile again.

After he left, Hannah told me that she saw Candace's face when the plate broke. She said perhaps Candace bumped into me by accident, but was too embarrassed to admit it. I'm not so sure.

## PJ

Don't want to let the Q-Crew down. Need to take time to look for wire cutters. Mo needs help. I've been having too much fun. Falling down on the job. Can't watch for people leaving early, even though I said I would. My schedule has been so tight that I'm always the one who leaves early!

I have talked to everyone about markers though. The only black markers I found were in the office.

## MO

I found One A-Chord! Beth was with me. We screamed and ran toward the cabin. I think it's a counselor's cabin, and it had the shades down and the door shut. We heard them singing inside. At first we listened. Then we pounded on the door until Elias Greer came from behind us and made us leave the front porch. The music stopped, and everything was completely quiet. I am so excited! At least I know now where they're staying! They're in Cabin #26!

## JAKE

PJ has been the first one in and the last one out of the cafeteria for every meal since we got here. And he eats the entire time. I hope he has room left for what's coming.

## MO

I heard One A-Chord again. This time I was walking by the kitchen toward the cafeteria. I could not mistake their unique sound. They were singing quietly, probably so no one would find them. I casually wandered up to the kitchen's back door and tiptoed in. I was so excited! I didn't want to scare them away. My heart was pounding. What would I say? Would they be as wonderful in real life as they are on their music videos?

# Chapter Eighteen

# An Afternoon of Surprises

## JAKE

Braden has a mild case of poison ivy. I don't know how he got it. Braden probably didn't stay on the paths. The counselors are always warning us not to wander off the paths for this very reason. Braden doesn't seem much like someone who likes to wander around the woods though. When the rest of us in the cabin went on a hike, he stayed by the lake and read a book. He probably found the only patch of poison ivy around here. Too bad. He looks miserable. I'm almost glad that I didn't get in any good running time. I'd hate to be in his predicament. He says he'll still play in the competition.

## IZZY

Candace came up to me at lunchtime. She admitted that she was really sorry about breaking my plate. It was an accident.

Then she asked me to come with her. We walked over to PJ's table, and Candace apologized, just like that. She said she was sorry for all the mean things she said about him on the bus. She wasn't joking around, either. I looked at her and could not believe what I had heard. All I could say was, "But it's not Friday yet!"

Candace nodded. She said we are all in the same youth group and should be on the same team. Then she mentioned all the vandalism and said, "Find out who's doing it, Izzy." She left me standing there with my mouth hanging open. Will wonders never cease!

## MO

My heart dropped to my stomach when I realized my mistake. The kitchen staff was listening to a One A-Chord CD. How could I have fallen for that? Then I had an awful gut feeling that things were about to get worse.

## PJ

I couldn't believe it. Candace actually apologized to me. Said she didn't mean to say all those rotten things about me during the bus ride up here. Asked me to be her partner in a sack race. That was really strange. Stuck my hand into my pocket and found a grasshopper. Now how did that get in there? It spit brown slimy stuff all over me and hopped away. Went to the bathhouse to wash it off. I felt really bad. Saw Mr. Greer carrying the last two pots out. Had to follow him to see where he was putting them. Thought I should have helped him. I wished I'd come sooner. I felt awful! I left to find Izzy and Mo. Want to have it out with them. I have to know what's been going on.

## MO

Sad to say, my hunch was right. I trudged back to Cabin #26, and the door was slightly ajar. There were sheets, pillows, blankets, soap and all sorts of cleaning supplies. Obviously it's a storage cabin. In one corner was a radio. One of the camp cats was sitting on top of it. Wrong again. How depressing!

What was worse, I saw PJ heading back toward the cafeteria. I had to keep him from seeing what the others were doing inside. He's been ignoring us all week. We thought he'd be busy with a craft or something. I rushed over and tried to get him into a conversation about the latest computer technologies. I had no idea what I was talking about! He must not have either. I think I totally confused him. PJ said he wanted to know what was going on.

What I want to know is how he could have suspected!

## JAKE

I glanced out the window and saw that Mo was losing the battle with PJ. I ran out and told him that some kids were snitch hunting down at the lake. He took off immediately! I didn't tell him that the snitch hunting gag is an old camp trick. Of course, there's no such thing.

PJ was so mad when he came back! But his snitch hunting gave us just enough time. When he burst into the cafeteria, we were all hiding behind chairs.

## PJ

I should have known. The Q-Crew are great friends. The best. With all the activities at camp, I lost track of the date. I completely forgot what today is. They threw a surprise birthday party for me! We had chocolate cake, ice cream, balloons, games and everything. Lou helped arrange it with the camp. The whole youth group was there. Candace even gave me a baseball cap with the camp's name on it. Said it would protect my face from the sun. Lots of new friends came, too.

## MO

Elias Greer can't be our suspect. He was so sweet!! He gave PJ a pot of petunias to help him remember the camp experience. And a couple of giant candy bars. Maybe Mr. Greer was trying to cover for himself, but I don't think so. There's something about him that makes me like him after all. I can't quite put my finger on it.

All the kids are beginning to talk about their favorite part of camp. I don't have a favorite part so far this year. I've hardly done anything except practice and look for One A-Chord. That's pretty sad.

## JAKE

Boy, I'm sure glad that I found out about Mr. Greer. I'm seeing him in a whole new light. He was really nice at PJ's party.

I still wonder why he's so grumpy most of the time, though. Maybe he's a frustrated musician and wishes he could be out there performing instead of digging in the dirt all summer long. I wonder if he knows he's good enough to be a professional.

The cake prank we played on PJ worked great. We set out a cardboard box that was frosted like a real cake. His face was hilarious when he cut into it. He was laughing so hard that I took the knife away from him before he cut himself. Then Izzy brought out the real cake. I ate three pieces. It's a good thing Grandma's not around to find out.

## MO

During PJ's party, I was thinking about what a different camp experience this has been. Usually by this time of the week, I have woven baskets, gone on horseback rides, shot archery arrows and done just about every activity the counselors plan. Between practicing and following my One A-Chord leads, I've hardly had any camp fun at all!

After Candace apologized to Izzy, I felt that I owed my friends an apology. I've been too busy to spend time with them. Good old PJ smiled and told me that it wasn't too late. He has been going so fast and furious that he'd signed up for at least eight activities a day. I'd been too busy to have any fun, and he had been too busy having fun to really enjoy it. We laughed about it.

Just then, Beth came and got me. She had a lead on One A-Chord!

Chapter Nineteen

# Famous Footsteps

## IZZY

We went out to a meadow and had a water balloon fight, the boys against the girls. I personally was going after the boys, like we should have been doing. Candace, on the other hand, went after me. I think it was her way of trying to make it up to me for being so mean. So I went after her, too. We were both soaked to the skin. It was almost like we were friends.

After the party, we were all throwing each other into the lake. It was great. This whole experience has brought us all closer, and I believe that I have learned a whole lot about thinking before I give an opinion. It's an awful thought, but I almost owe Candace thanks.

## PJ

After the water balloon fight, we went swimming. I let them throw me in, kind of a "birthday boy" thing. I can't remember having more fun. Camp is awesome.

Ouch! My sunburn hurts. I like the cap Candace gave me, but I think it's too late to save my face. Should have used that sunscreen she gave me. I guess we missed the sack races, but that's okay. It was a fantastic birthday party! I can't wait to tell Mom and Pris about it. I missed having them there. But it was still one of the best birthdays in my entire life!

## JAKE

Gerard of the Jingle Singers had his instrument egged. I don't like the way this is heading. They don't know if they'll be able to clean it off in time for the competition. It might even be ruined. They reported the incident to the counselors.

## IZZY

I was surprised to find that one girl from our youth group actually wanted someone to pull a prank on her. She sighed and said, "Camp is so much more exciting when there are a lot of pranks going on."

I had an opinion on that, and I could finally express it. I asked where in the world she has been for the last few days. Of course, kids who aren't in a band might not have heard about all the things that have been happening. So I asked her in a nice way.

Everyone is taking this vandalism problem really well. It's getting pretty personal though. If it gets too much worse, I wonder if the head counselors will send us home. No one's been hurt yet, but a lot of things have been almost ruined.

## MO

Beth said that the practice cabin would be closed for an hour for cleaning. All those pranks have messed it up. But what a perfect cover for One A-Chord to get in some practice! They are so tricky. They knew everyone would be swimming and wouldn't be able to hear them practicing. But I have them figured out. They'll be there, and we'll be waiting!

## IZZY

I talked to Lou about all the vandalism. The counselors think that there are a lot more pranks going on during this week's camp than usual. They're convinced that they are innocent pranks though. Nothing has been serious, although some have been done in poor taste. I beg to differ with them on what has been done to the instruments. Those incidents were downright vandalism and not pranks.

The camp has decided to have counselors walk around and patrol the camp at night. Lou said they would make an announcement at dinner to discourage the pranksters. I am so glad that something is going to be done.

I had to laugh when Lou mentioned that they would look the other way if PJ did a prank. They are getting such a kick out of how many ways he can sort potted petunias. Of all of them, I guess Mr. Greer is getting the biggest kick out of it.

Chapter Twenty

# A New Suspect

## MO

After eating some birthday cake, Beth and I waited behind a bush on the side of the practice cabin. We hid under an open window so we'd hear One A-Chord when they came in. We waited there for over half an hour. Beth was complaining about leg cramps. My neck was stiff. But it was worth it. At any minute, One A-Chord would be setting up their instruments inside. Then we heard footsteps inside the cabin near the open window above us. It sounded like someone was carrying something heavy. Like instruments!

Suddenly, a bucketful of dirty wash water flew out the window and spilled all over our heads.

I can't believe it! Why would you close a cabin to clean it and then really clean it? So much for Beth's great lead!

## PJ

The counselors are getting more strict about letting us go out at night. How can I do anything? Will have to think about this. I've come up with such a great prank that I have to pull it off. I may have to change it slightly.

I did have good news at mail call! I got five letters and three of them weren't even from me! Mom and Pris wrote to say happy birthday. And Mr. Potter wrote to say he hoped I was having a terrific time at camp. Totally stupendous!

## JAKE

Chapel tonight was on faithfulness. We're musicians. We understand how important it is to be faithful. We have to be faithful to practice and take care of our instruments. I couldn't help but wonder about something. What if I were as faithful to God as I am to my music? He certainly deserves my faithfulness more than my guitar does.

## MO

Faithfulness. God is faithful to us. I can be faithful to God. Great fruit of the Spirit! It's my favorite!

## IZZY

It was so humid tonight. My hair curled up even tighter than it normally does. When the rain started pouring, it was no surprise.

# PJ

We were jamming tonight. Saw some of the Royal Rhythmics and Jingle Singers standing out in the rain. Mo knows Gerard from the Jingle Singers. She asked if they wanted to join us. I asked the Rhythmics. Don't know them, but they came on in. One of the Royal Rhythmics, Tabitha, had a cut guitar string. Jake gave her one of his. Got to playing really hard. Drowned out the thunder. No one realized when the storm stopped. Mo almost beat her drums to a pulp. It was a blast!

Gave us a chance to get to know those other kids, too! They're not just competition, they're musicians just like us. Was disappointed when our nine o'clock curfew came around. Decided I wanted a quick look at the sound equipment, so went to my cabin by way of the stage. Something caught my eye right on top of the sound cabinet. I picked up a cut guitar string. Wire cutters were right there, too. I tried to make sense of this. Could Travis be our vandal?

# MO

PJ caught up with us and told us about finding the wire cutters. I already suspected the sound man! He could be the one sabotaging the bands! It's often the quiet ones that you have to watch. Or at least that's what I tell everyone. That way I don't get blamed for everything that gets broken.

The sky is black tonight, too cloudy to see any stars. But everything feels so fresh! I breathed deeply to try and pull it all in. I love being outside after rain!

We got to the cabin and the clouds started looking threatening again. I decided to give the pranks a rest for one night.

## PJ

Lou made us take off our muddy shoes. Left them on the covered porch of our cabin. All the cabins were doing that. Guess the counselors got together and decided they didn't want mud inside. It gave me a great idea for pulling off two pranks in one night.

It looked like it could rain again. So I stayed awake until everyone was asleep. Then I slipped outside and put my shoes back on. Don't think Lou suspected anything. I can be quiet when I need to be. I looked around for counselors. Didn't see any.

Found a wheelbarrow and started collecting potted petunias. Rolled them over to the chapel. Decided that a chapel prank was okay. Just this once. Thursday morning's topic will be gentleness. What's more gentle than petunia petals?

Finished the job. On the way back, stopped at six cabin porches and tied everyone's shoelaces together. Then tied them to other people's shoes. Never saw a counselor. Perfect night for pranks. Made it back inside just before a downpour.

## JAKE

What a night we had! I woke up around midnight to the cracking and crackling of a terrible thunderstorm. The thunder and lightning were incredible! I opened the curtains and watched the show. It made me jump several times. Wind rocked the cabin and tore at the trees. It kept me awake most of the night. A couple other guys woke up and watched the storm with me. PJ slept right through it. I guess staying up pulling pranks the past couple of nights wore him out. I wonder what crazy prank he had to skip tonight because of the rain.

## MO

It was the weirdest thing. I woke up this morning and did not feel like searching for One A-Chord. What a shocker! At first, I thought I must be sick. I felt my forehead. No fever.

Then I figured out what was wrong with me. Or right with me. I finally realized how many camp activities I had given up. And for what? For nothing! I missed having fun in order to meet some people who might not even be here. What was I thinking? It was time to get myself under control. I decided to start keeping a schedule like PJ's. And I'll help set a trap for Travis. I have lots of catching up to do!

## IZZY

What an awful storm. The wind even blew through cracks in the cabin. I was so glad to be within cabin walls on a night like last night. It would have been dreadful to be in a tent. The rain made the air smell clean though. It was a gorgeous morning!! I decided to take a walk before breakfast. That's when I saw him.

## Chapter Twenty-One

# Jake's Discovery

### IZZY

Elias Greer was looking down at a flower bed on Thursday morning as if he were in complete shock. He looked incredibly sad. At his feet, instead of his dainty petunias and marigolds, were pieces of flowers, stems and even roots. I can't believe what I saw. That terrible storm ruined his garden! In fact, it ruined nearly every flower in every flower bed in the camp. I feel so sorry for Mr. Greer.

### JAKE

When I saw the flower beds this morning, I felt awful. The storm did the kind of damage that I had wanted to do to get back at Mr. Greer. Only worse. I went over to his cabin and offered to help him replant the flower beds. I figured it was the least I could do. I even confessed to him what I had almost done. He seemed shocked, but he forgave me for thinking of hurting him that way.

At first, he wasn't going to let me help. He said I should enjoy the last couple days at camp. Then I told him that I had loads of experience working with my grandfather in my grandmother's garden. He accepted my help. He said that with two experienced gardeners working together, we'd have the flower beds replanted in no time. I wasn't sure I liked being called a gardener, but I guess I can overlook it just this once.

As soon as Mr. Greer gets back from town with new plants and we finish competing in the semifinals, we'll start replanting. None of us have come up with a plan to trap Travis yet, but we're keeping our eyes on him.

## IZZY

I checked our instruments in the practice cabin right away. I had to make sure that the roof didn't leak and that everything was okay. Last night's storm was so horrible. Everything checked out fine, even though I did discover one wet spot on the floor near the door. I didn't find anything wrong with the instruments or our music. I guess the storm and patrolling counselors kept the vandals away, too.

## MO

What a wonderful surprise we had at chapel today! It was beautiful! Someone put potted petunias all around the podium and there were plants up and down the aisles. I hope PJ didn't get too wet out in that storm last night.

The speaker talked about gentleness. The tender petals on the potted petunias and the vicious storm last night gave him perfect illustrations. He contrasted the two. It gave me a lot to think about. God is gentle with us and wants us to treat other people with gentleness too. Gentleness is definitely the fruit of the Spirit that I need most. It could well be my favorite!

## PJ

They noticed! Everyone seemed to like the petunias at chapel. I can say with confidence that it was a semi-successful prank. It wasn't totally successful, because a couple kids that I didn't even know came up to me and said "Nice job." Of course I acted like I didn't know what they were talking about. It's all a part of being the camp prankster. You have to keep your identity a secret.

What was really successful was the shoelace tying. It was so funny watching people trying to get their shoelaces untied. I had to force myself to keep from laughing out loud. To cover, I tied my own last night too. Couldn't get them untied. Had to shuffle around with tied shoes. Only made it funnier. Finally, Lou noticed my dilemma and helped me get the knots untied. No one had a clue who did the shoelace tying. I'm getting the hang of this.

## JAKE

PJ is so funny. I wonder if he realizes that his chapel "prank" saved all the potted petunias in the camp. Lou told me that Elias Greer was so grateful that PJ had done it. The counselors decided to overlook his shoelace-tying escapade. Except for PJ, they have a no tolerance policy for even innocent pranksters because things have gone too far.

I don't think anyone would have suspected PJ of tying the shoelaces except that he kept saying, "Even mine are tied. Who could have done this?" Then he would give a silly grin, which gave him away. He is just not a prankster.

Have to get ready for the semifinals. After everything that has happened this week, I wonder what surprises we have in store.

## IZZY

After all that's happened, I was amazed at how well we played today in the semifinals. Our instruments were clean. Jake's guitar strings were in place. PJ's voice didn't sound like it was changing, and Mo hit all the beats in correct time.

We sang and played our songs just the way we used to before all this sabotaging stuff took place. It was great.

Just outside the door, Mr. Greer was tending some potted plants that escaped the storm. He seemed to have reflective look on his face. He's gruff, but he has a very gentle heart. He's a better example of gentleness than I thought a few days ago.

A question keeps plaguing me. What would Travis have to gain by sabotaging instruments?

## JAKE

I wonder what happened to Travis. He didn't do anything to disrupt the semifinals. Everyone's instruments were okay, and

Travis ran the soundboard perfectly. Maybe locking the practice cabin and having counselors patrol the grounds made the difference. What a relief!

We made it into the finals. So did the Royal Rhythmics, the Jammers, the Heavenly Harpers, Angel Wings, the O's, His Majesty's Minstrels, and the Jingle Singers. Even though all of those bands are really good, I think we have a decent chance of winning.

## PJ

Braden played well. Even though everyone's afraid to go near him. Afraid to catch poison ivy. All except Lance. Says he's not allergic to it. I am, so I steered clear. Don't want anything to spoil my camp experience.

Found a cricket in my pocket today. I can't help but wonder if someone is planting these animals and insects in my pockets. It's such an odd thing. I still miss my frog friend.

## MO

I think it was rude for One A-Chord not to show up to listen to the semifinals. None of the counselors did either. I found out later that the counselors weren't allowed to listen because they know the kids too well. The judges were the people who work in the office and a lady who plays the organ at a local church.

I'm running out of time here. I've given up so much of my camp time to find One A-Chord.

## IZZY

Listening pays off. I hung around after the semifinals and observed. Then a girl from Angel Wings ran up to Travis and gave him a hug. She called him Uncle Travis.

## JAKE

Mr. Greer had already started replanting when we finished the semifinals. I had to change into grubby clothes. When I got back, we started working near the door. He had lots of bags of dry peat moss and topsoil to fill in where the dirt had washed away. Good thing. Otherwise we would have had to wait until the soil dried out. Gardeners know that you don't work in wet soil. But it was important to get the camp looking nice again before Friday.

At first, we didn't talk. Finally, Mr. Greer spoke up. He apologized for getting on me so much. He also admitted that he needed to try to be more patient. And he said he would try to stop yelling and talk more softly. I figured he must have heard the chapel speech today on gentleness.

The New Valley Noisemakers decided to get in some extra practice before lunch. I don't know why. They didn't make the finals. Every time they screeched out a high note or the trumpet player played wrong notes, I saw Mr. Greer wince. It was almost as if he felt pain somewhere.

Then I realized that it must get old having to listen all day to kids who are practically tone deaf singing and playing instruments. Especially for someone like Mr. Greer who plays so well. At least the campers can get away from it. With his cabin right nearby, Mr. Greer is stuck having to listen to kids playing most of the time. If I had to do that, I'd be grumpy too.

## PJ

I had a hunch about how Travis could sneak in and out without being caught. We all know that he has a key to the cabin, but he had to have a hidden route to get there unnoticed. Started back toward the practice cabin to check on it. Took a shortcut through the woods. Wish I hadn't. There went my perfect week of camp.

Chapter Twenty-Two

# PJ in the Soup

## PJ

Met a skunk. Now I know why cartoon characters run from skunks. Everyone was running from me, too. I wished I could have run away from myself. Skunk odors don't go away. Lou's shower rule isn't good enough for guys who meet up with skunks.

They have a special soap and shampoo for getting rid of skunk smell. But the camp was out of it. Can you believe that? They had plenty of tomato juice though. It came in really handy.

Had to soak in a big sink. In tomato juice. Had to wash my hair in it too. A couple of the guys came in and said it looked like I was in a pot of spaghetti sauce. They threw in some noodles. Very funny.

## IZZY

Mo and I decided to help Mr. Greer and Jake plant new petunias and marigolds. PJ couldn't come since he was up to his ears in tomatoes.

Mr. Greer showed us how to prepare the soil, plant and then water each flower.

Replanting flowers sure takes a lot longer than I expected. My fingers and nails were getting filthy. I was afraid that I wouldn't be able to get them clean. So I asked Mr. Greer if he had some gardening gloves I could use. He told me where to look in the potting shed. I asked for the key, and he said it was always unlocked.

## MO

When Izzy went to find some gloves, I figured it was a good time to try to get some information from Mr. Greer about where One A-Chord might be staying. I was getting ready to talk about them when I noticed that he looked grumpy again.

I don't know which band was playing, but they were completely out of sync with one another. Their music had almost an eerie sound to it. Mr. Greer did not look like he was in the mood for a conversation. At first, I didn't think I should question him. But I realized it could be my only chance, so I started right in.

Elias Greer didn't say much, but I had the strong feeling that he knew more than he was telling me. I was in the middle of interrogating him when he had a coughing fit or something. He said he had to go get more plants. He left so fast that he was almost running.

Funny thing was, we still had at least six dozen flowers left to plant. He knows something. He just doesn't want to tell me. I'm sure of it.

## PJ

Had a lot of time to think in the sink. It wasn't actually a sink. It was a tub. Decided that Travis needs to be stopped. Knew we needed to know more about him. Lou would be our best source.

Fortunately, Lou came in to check on me. I asked him about Travis. Lou said that Travis lives in a nearby town. He goes to the same church as the woman who helped judge the semi-finals. He's here during the day for us and then goes home at night. He doesn't come back until around ten A.M.

If he leaves, how can he do pranks at night? I guess that means it's probably not him, but I know what I saw. Something isn't right here.

## MO

My head was down and my hands were in the dirt. Then I heard it! It sounded like the laugh I've heard from Mackenzie Sutton in an interview. I tried to locate the person who had made that laugh, but couldn't. I gave up and went back to planting.

After my unsuccessful interrogation, Mr. Greer left Izzy and me to work on the west side of the building. He worked with Jake on the east side. Izzy wasn't talking much, so I thought about the week. I knew I had to find a way to stay focused. After all, this is camp! I'm supposed to be doing camp things, not chasing after the elusive One A-Chord. (Izzy taught me that word. I love it! I stretch it out and say ee-looo-sive! Sounds elegant and mysterious at the same time.)

Planting flowers was actually kind of fun. I especially liked how pretty it looked when we finished each section. Izzy and I finished our side of the cabin. Mr. Greer told us to go enjoy ourselves. I took him up on it. I have a lot of fun time to make up!

## JAKE

Mr. Greer and I took a break. He had a jug of cold lemonade with him. He thanked me for helping him and said that gardening is always more fun when you do it with a friend.

That surprised me. He called me a friend. After a couple hours of working alone with him, I liked him. He was listening to me talk about the Q-Crew and all the adventures we've had together. He even told me a little about his own life. Especially when he was my age. He was in a band too. I told him that I thought he had real talent, and he should have stayed in a band.

Every now and then he would wet a cloth with water from the hose and put it over his eyes and forehead. I think he had a headache or something. I felt sorry for him.

## MO

Okay, maybe One A-Chord is here at camp. Maybe they've outwitted Detective Mo, but I have to somehow keep myself from trying to find them. I don't want to miss out on any more camp activities. I asked Izzy to help me control myself. She agreed. It's nice to have the old, opinionated Izzy back. I need her! I wish she had been there to tell me to stop all this nonsense. I need to experience all that camp has to offer. I've got to stop obsessing (another Izzy word) over One A-Chord.

I made my first step. I went up to Travis and asked him what he used wire cutters for. He showed me the types of repairs he has to do on the sound equipment. He said that he wanted to fix something a couple of days ago, but his wire cutters were missing. He admitted that he's not very organized with his stuff. He finally found the wire cutters yesterday—right where he thought he'd left them. He figured that they were covered with papers or something when he tried to find them before. I believe him. He's disorganized. Anyone can see that! Izzy agrees.

Right now, I'm going to go to three activities in the next two hours. If PJ can do it, then I can, too!

## IZZY

Mo and I discussed Travis as a suspect. It seems to us that if he were really the vandal, then he wouldn't have left the evidence on his own sound cabinet. And he wouldn't have admitted to owning the wire cutters. He didn't defend himself even once. I don't even think he has a motive. I've been listening to a rehearsal, and the Angel Wings band is good enough to win without his help. No, Travis is clean. As soon as I see Jake and PJ, I'm going to tell them that Travis is no longer a suspect.

## PJ

Jake told me what Mo found out. Glad Travis isn't the one. Good thing Jake told me before Travis came to visit me in the tub. I was completely surprised when I saw him take out his earplugs. What kind of a sound man uses earplugs? I sure hope he doesn't use them during the competition.

Before he left, Travis mentioned that his wire cutters are missing again. I'd been in the tub quite a while. Got used to it. Was enjoying the visitors. But with the wire cutters missing again, it was time for me to get out.

Figured the skunk smell was gone. Visitors stopped holding their noses. Got out of the tub fast. Had to take a shower and then tell the others.

## Chapter Twenty-Three

# More Bad News

### IZZY

We played a game of capture the flag. It was so much fun. For a change, Candace and I were on the same side. I can almost see why some people like her. She had a plan. It was a great plan for capturing the other team's flag. Jake and Tim went for the flag while Hannah and I created a diversion. By the time their team had taken us to jail, our team had the flag. It was unbelievable. We were all grinning and laughing. This is how it should be. I wish it were like this all of the time.

### MO

Capture the flag gave me a great idea! I told the others about it. They said it was brilliant, of course! We're going to take shifts tonight and keep our eyes open for pranksters.

I remember seeing other people's shadows the first two nights when I was out. They probably belonged to the vandals. We'll be ready for them tonight. Of course, the counselors will be out, too, so we're going to have to be extra careful. They told us we have to have an exceptionally good reason to be out at night.

## IZZY

After the game, a bunch of us went to the practice cabin to get our instruments ready for the finals tomorrow. Candace came too. We stood side by side staring at the mess. I can't believe that the vandals would strike in broad daylight! All five guitars leaning against the wall in the practice cabin had their strings cut.

Suddenly, the guitarists moved forward, even the ones whose strings were not cut. Guitar strings came out of cases and everyone helped everyone else restring their instruments. I hope that no one breaks another string. There aren't going to be any strings left.

The Heavenly Harpers' drummer found his drumsticks broken, and His Majesty's Minstrels found sand in a flute. The Jammers found one of their drums outside covered with dirt. Someone even poured syrup on the O's keyboard. I would be livid. I think that that might ruin it. I've decided to take my keyboard to my cabin tonight. There isn't much room, but I'll sleep with it if I have to. I can't risk someone pouring syrup on my keyboard.

I really hope we can find the culprits. This has gotten way out of hand.

## MO

It looks like guitars belonging to Heavenly Harpers, Jake, Jingle Singers, Angel Wings and Royal Rythmics were hit. Jake used all of his strings and even had to borrow one from someone else. The strange thing was how quiet it was in the building even though we were all in there!

The O's were so discouraged that they wanted to quit the competition. But we all talked them out of it. Izzy told them that they could use her keyboard. Gerard said that the Jingle Singers have decided to sing acappella. They figure that if they don't use instruments, then the vandals can't hurt them.

## JAKE

We had our last rehearsal. I don't think we've ever played better. Lots of other musicians were waiting for their turn. I saw Lance whispering something to Braden. I think he's worried that we might beat them. The counselors are upset. What happened to the instruments today changed their minds. They finally realized that these are not just pranks. If the finals weren't tomorrow, the camp would cancel the competition. That's what Lou told me. There will be lots of counselors out tonight patrolling the grounds. If they catch anyone out, that person will be sent home. No questions asked.

## PJ

Another great mail call! Got six letters. Two weren't from me! Mom and Pris are great to keep writing me.

Chapel tonight was on self-control. A little late, I think. Things have been out of control around here all week.

## MO

I can honestly say that self-control is not my favorite fruit of the Spirit. It's a hard one. I'm learning a lot about self-control this week, though. Who knows? By the end of the week it might be my favorite. JAKE

I asked Lou about PJ. Lou smiled and said that they were making an exception for PJ. I asked if he thought I should go with PJ to help keep him safe. He thought that would be a good idea. Told the girls that it was too risky to have them out. He also said PJ and I have to be really quick. From the tone of his voice, I know he means it.

## PJ

I have a new favorite dessert called banana boats. We made them tonight at the campfire. You make a slit in the banana the long way and stuff some chocolate chips and marshmallows into the skin. Then you squeeze it closed, wrap it in foil and cook it on the fire till the chocolate and marshmallows melt. It was awesome!

Relieved the day is over. Glad to be out of the tomato juice and in a warm bed writing in my journal. I wish we had found those wire cutters. What if the vandals strike again?

## Chapter Twenty-Four

# An Eerie Night Out

### PJ

Who would have guessed it? My being a prankster has come in handy! Jake explained how much the counselors have enjoyed my pranks. I never would have guessed. They didn't show it. I'm allowed to do a prank again tonight. But Jake has to be with me.

Told Jake that it looks like another rainstorm is coming in. We're going to go out right after the rain stops.

Since One A-Chord and our parents are coming tomorrow for the concert, I decided that the potted petunias should go out along the driveway tonight. The wind is blowing a little, but I figure the pots will be all right. Won't everyone be surprised in the morning? What a good prank. Just have to wait for the weather to clear.

## JAKE

Woke PJ up. It was about three A.M. The storm had finally stopped. Lou had to help me wake him, but then he jumped back into his bed before PJ realized he had helped. I wonder how PJ has been getting up on his own all week. He sleeps like a log.

## MO

I hate waiting. I couldn't get to sleep knowing the boys were out there doing something with petunias. What if the vandals weren't satisfied with just damaging instruments? What if they wanted to hurt Jake and PJ? I felt so helpless until I remembered that I could be praying for them. I could also be praying that the culprits get caught.

## IZZY

I woke up in the middle of the night and peeked out of the cabin window. It looked so dark. Susan came to stand next to me. After a while, she told me that Jake and PJ would be okay. She said the other counselors would be watching out for them. I smiled at her. How did she know what I was thinking?

## JAKE

PJ wanted me to turn my back while he did his prank. Like I didn't know that he was going to move the petunias from the chapel to somewhere else. I convinced him that if we both worked together, we could work slower and keep our eyes out for other pranksters.

Lou had told me that as long as each one of us had a

petunia pot in our hands, we were safe. The other counselors would recognize us immediately. Made sure I kept one in my hands at all times.

## PJ

We lined the road with petunias. Jake suggested putting a few by the practice cabin so that we could check it out. There was double the amount of potted petunias around here. When I mentioned it, Jake said that Mr. Greer bought a bunch more. He wants the camp looking nice when the parents come.

We took as long as we dared. But we finally had to go back in.

One last note for the night. The night plays tricks on the eyes. We didn't go as far as the field, but from far away the field looked like a field of white. I've never noticed that before. Must be comfortable enough being a prankster that I'm noticing things now. Or maybe all the rain made it look that way.

Put a pot on the porch of each cabin. The place looked great. Only wish we had found a suspect. We were exhausted when we went back to bed. We needed sleep to do well at the finals. Think I'll skip breakfast.

## MO

When Jake and PJ put a pot of petunias on our porch, I tried to slip outside. Susan stopped me. She said to let PJ have his day. I was disappointed, but I knew she was right. It's so hard waiting!

## JAKE

I'm glad we didn't try having the whole Q-Crew out here. There were counselors everywhere. They tried to stay out of the way. We would have been in big trouble without petunias in our hands.

As we put the last pots of petunias on our cabin porch and went to bed, I wondered how late the counselors would be out. If I were the culprit, I would have waited until just after dawn. The counselors probably won't patrol once it gets light out. They'll be exhausted. I'm going to try to wake up early.

## JAKE

I overslept this morning and didn't wake up early to patrol the campground. But I woke up feeling great about today's competition. Even with everything that's happened, I know the Q-Crew is ready. All we can do is play our best. It's off to breakfast and then on to the competition.

## IZZY

Jake is breathing fire! And I'm having a hard time not knocking someone over the head. It was raining when we went to sleep last night. When we got up for breakfast, a soccer field of white greeted us. But it wasn't snow. Spread out over the grass-covered field were sopping-wet papers. I picked one up. It was page three of the music for our song "Horizon." It tore apart in my hand. On further investigation, we found out that all of our music had been spread out in the field and rained on. All of it. There wasn't a page left.

# JAKE

I don't know what to do. The finals are in a few hours. The big concert is tonight. Our parents are coming. We have no music. I can't think straight.

I offered to help Mr. Greer finish up in the garden. I might complain a lot about garden work, but right then I knew that I needed to keep my hands busy to help me calm down. I didn't have to explain. Mr. Greer seemed to understand.

We set to work on the garden by the practice cabin. We worked our way to the back of the cabin. There was a mess of overgrown grasses and weeds around the bushes under the window. We decided to clean them out.

Suddenly, out of the corner of my eye, I noticed it. I grabbed Mr. Greer's arm just in time.

Chapter Twenty-Five

# A Prank to Dye For

## JAKE

Mr. Greer didn't see the telltale signs. He was at the wrong angle. But I saw them clearly. Dark green, shiny leaves in sets of three. Just under the window and hidden by tall grass and weeds was a patch of poison ivy.

## PJ

Jake pulled me aside after breakfast. I meant to sleep in, but my stomach started growling. Came to breakfast late.

Told me about the poison ivy. After eating, we ran back to the practice cabin. Checked the storage room at the back. That's where our instruments were put on Monday. Campers aren't supposed to use it.

The door wasn't locked this time. Didn't know there was a

window in there. It was unlocked. There were streaks in the dust on the windowsill. Someone had been there recently. On the floor just inside the window was Lance's missing capo.

Hard keeping my mouth shut. We had a Q-Crew meeting.

## IZZY

The answer was so clear. The Jammers have been climbing in the window on the south side of the practice cabin to do all of their stunts. The Jammers look like such angels on the outside. I wouldn't even want to guess at what they look like on the inside.

When Braden had a mild case of poison ivy, I should have known. Of course, I didn't know that there was poison ivy there, but I should have known. Where is my women's intuition when I need it? I guess I was so busy paying attention to Candace that I didn't think things through.

## MO

Met with the Q-Crew. We jumped to conclusions with Mr. Greer and Travis. We sure didn't want to do that again!

I should have suspected Lance and Braden the moment Lance spiked poor Hannah with the volleyball. That showed his true colors. I was too busy to put clues together. I even saw their shadows on Monday and Tuesday nights as I was doing my pranks. They were tall shadows. Why didn't I put two and two together sooner? We should have all known! And Mr. Greer keeps the potting shed unlocked. They had access to fresh dirt!

I have a new plan. No one liked it much. But I decided to try it anyway. I think Mr. Greer will help me. Maybe it will work.

## JAKE

We decided to try something risky. I took Lance's capo over to him. He was happy to get it back and asked where I found it. When I told him, he got very pale. He said he guessed someone stole it and left it there.

I shook my head and told him that I had another theory. Maybe he lost it one of the times he happened to climb into the storage closet window right by the poison ivy…which he isn't allergic to.

His eyes got all skinny. I told him that it seemed to me that the closet window was a good way to sneak into the cabin without being seen. Then it would be easy for him and his cohorts to sabotage the instruments of any band they saw as a threat. He didn't say anything. He stuck the capo in his pocket, turned around and walked away. He knew that I knew. It was my way of warning him to leave our stuff alone.

## IZZY

Now that I think about it, the Jammers are the only ones who have had nothing damaged. One found his instrument in the bathhouse and another found his in the kitchen freezer. These were minor things to keep others from suspecting them. When everyone else's strings were cut, they had a drum in the dirt. That's not such a big deal. And although Braden said his string was cut earlier in the week, all PJ ever saw was that Braden was changing his guitar string.

## MO

Mr. Greer was great! Happy to help. He says it's a long shot, but maybe we'll catch the vandals red-handed. Or green. Or purple.

## PJ

This has taken me totally by surprise! Except for this last bit, I never saw a single clue. Wow! And I was so impressed with Braden. He lied to me the entire time, and I believed him! How could I have been so gullible? I was concentrating too much on having fun at camp to see what was going on!

## IZZY

I told the others that I would report the Jammers to the administration. They tried to dissuade me. I know that it will look like we're trying to remove them from the competition so that we can win. I'm sure that it will seem malicious. But no matter how it appears, I know this is the right thing. The others realized it too. Mo said she would go with me. I was glad. It was a very hard thing to do.

## MO

I can't believe it! The head counselors said that all we had was circumstantial evidence! Braden could have gotten poison ivy in another place. The real vandals could have left Lance's capo in the storage closet. We felt so stupid. We're still sure that the Jammers are guilty. It's so frustrating! We need proof. I wonder if my plan will work, and we can get the proof in time.

## IZZY

I'm so upset. My stomach is tied in knots, and it is all I can do not to go over and start yelling at the Jammers. But then maybe they didn't do it. Should I give them the benefit of the doubt? Why am I kidding myself? I know they did it. Temper, Izzy. Temper.

## MO

How can everything go so wrong all in one day?! This could have been one of the most important days of my life, but now, it's one of the worst. The Jammers didn't just ruin our music. Now we have another problem. Jake found his guitar strings cut. All of them. They had to have been cut after breakfast. He has no more. He doesn't know of anyone who does. And the finals start in less than an hour. There isn't time to find a store in town and buy some strings even if Lou could drive him there.

What can we do? I want to climb a tree to think, but the bark is too wet and slippery. I'm not going to do something stupid. But I do feel like doing something really mean and rotten. Oooh! They make me so mad!

## PJ

Everyone is getting set up for the finals at the stage down by the lake. We met at the practice cabin. Had to figure out what to do. Not fair. Not right. Couldn't believe Braden. Thought he was a friend. Felt like crying or yelling or something. Have to figure out what to do.

## JAKE

Boy, did I feel like getting revenge today! But I've finally calmed down. I had to. I took one good lap around the camp with Ginger at my side, and I realized that it wouldn't do us any good to stay angry. Grandma is always telling me not to cry over spilt milk. She grew up on a farm and likes to quote old sayings. I never really understood that one before. But I guess I do now. When you spill milk on the way from the barn to the kitchen, it soaks into the ground. You can't scoop it up and use it. It's gone forever. Crying about it won't help. Getting mad about it won't change anything. So basically, you have to deal with it.

Now it's impossible for our dream of winning to come true. We don't have all our instruments. We don't have music. The only thing we still have is the reason we play. We still have God. So we asked him to help us figure out what to do.

## IZZY

After we prayed, we decided to go to the stage and wait our turn. We didn't know what else we could do. We decided to get up there as a group and tell everyone what happened. We would all like to point a finger at the perpetrators, but we can't. This band was founded to give honor and glory to God. We have to honor him in bad times as well as in good times. We asked ourselves what Jesus would do in our situation. We know that he would forgive them. We asked God to give us wisdom to do the right thing, whatever that is.

## Chapter Twenty-Six

# The Show Goes On

### IZZY

The camp director, Mr. Tabb, made a surprise announcement. He said that the judging for today's final competition would have two parts. The winners will be chosen based on their musical and performance abilities as well as on how well they honor God in their attitudes and actions. He said that he wants to help us concentrate on what is important.

However, it's so easy to put on a big act and try to fool everyone. I wondered how the judges would be able to see through people's façades. I mean, sometimes I'm not even sure about myself. I have to examine my motives to make sure I'm really sincere. Often I know I'm just acting the way I think people want me to, because I'm trying to impress them or something. It's really hard to be yourself when people are watching you.

## PJ

Got to the stage. Everyone stopped and stared. They must have heard about our ruined music. Jake came in with his guitar. Looked awful with the broken strings hanging from it. Tried to borrow some. None to be found. Bummer!

## JAKE

It was so disgusting! I couldn't believe how holy and good the Jammers were acting when they performed. They wanted the prize, all right! Lance told everyone about what the Lord had been teaching him this week. He knew all the right words to say. He looked like an angel boy standing up there, all holy and good. Give me a break! Their performance was even better than usual.

The other bands all did a good job too. I could tell some of them were nervous knowing about the attitude part of the judging. I mean, who wouldn't be? I haven't exactly been perfect this week either.

## PJ

I was going through all our songs in my head. Maybe we could do them without music. But all I have to do is remember words and the tune. Everyone else plays an instrument and needs the notes. It seems pretty hopeless.

## IZZY

I can't stand watching all the phoniness going on. It's driving me crazy. That's why I have my diary with me now. If I keep writing in it, maybe I'll get my attitude under control. I know I can't get up there and not be myself. Not today. I don't want to be a phony.

That's why I need Jesus to help me all the time. I can't be perfect, no matter how hard I try! I can't always turn the other cheek and do good to my enemies. At least not without a huge amount of help from God.

## MO

The director's announcement put a whole new twist on everything. Suddenly the kids couldn't think just about playing the notes right. They had to remember to show how kind and patient and everything they could be. It's like when my brothers and I are yelling at one another and then my Aunt Marian comes into the room. We stop immediately and start acting nice. How can the competition judges tell who's faking it?

As I sat there watching the other groups, I asked God to help me. It was really hard knowing that we would not be able to compete. It was even harder knowing that my dream of playing before One A-Chord was dead forever. Gone! Kaput.

But then I remembered something really important. Actually, I think God reminded me. I play my drums because I love doing it. It's a way to express what I'm feeling deep inside. I enjoy bringing happiness to the people who listen. And I especially love playing for God. I like to praise him through my drumsticks. They carry a message from my heart straight to God's heart. And that's more important than winning.

## JAKE

I finally decided that the competition doesn't matter. Not really. What really matters is what's going on inside of me. I asked God to forgive me for the way I've been thinking and feeling about the Jammers. I asked him to help Lance and the others learn how much fun it is to play for God.

## PJ

They finally called us to the platform. Walked straight and tall with our heads high, even though we couldn't play. We didn't want God or our youth group to feel ashamed of us. Jake took the microphone and explained that we had decided not to compete.

Just then the Jammers' lead singer, Lance, ran up. He came onstage with Braden's guitar. Got on the mike and offered to let Jake use it. Of course, we all knew what he was up to.

## JAKE

I knew that Lance was trying to make himself look good so his band could win the prize. What a phony! Here he was acting all noble and everything, and he was probably the one who held the wire cutters that destroyed my strings. It made me sick.

But I had to make a choice. Right up on stage in front of everyone. I didn't want to be a hypocrite like Lance. I wanted to honor God with my actions, no matter what anyone thought. But we didn't even have music. I looked at Izzy, then Mo, then PJ. They each nodded in turn. As a group, we made the decision without speaking a word.

## Chapter Twenty-Seven

# Frogs and Lizards and Insects

## PJ

Knew what we had to do. Not a performance anymore. This was a battle. A battle between good and evil. I wanted to lay into Lance so badly. I felt like wrapping that guitar around his head. But I wanted to please God. I couldn't do both. So I took the microphone from Jake and waited for Izzy's cue.

## IZZY

I got behind the keyboard. I prayed silently for help. I wanted to play to give God glory. Otherwise there was no point in playing at all.

We hadn't even discussed what to play. But somehow I think we all knew. I hit the opening chord and the others joined in. Mo played quietly, reverently. Jake played only simple chords. He didn't do any of his fancy finger work. PJ sang the melody with a clear, strong voice and we all sang in harmony. "Holy, Holy, Holy! Lord God Almighty…."

## MO

It was like being part of a heavenly choir! This was one of the first songs we ever wrote. We knew it by heart. Somehow we all knew that it was the perfect one to sing right now.

## IZZY

We finished the song and there was silence in the room. Quietly, we all left the stage and sat down. Mr. Tabb took the platform. He prayed and thanked God for all the competitors and for how God had helped us grow this week. He prayed for everyone's safe return home tomorrow.

Then we got a shock. Mr. Tabb called Elias Greer to the podium. I wondered what on earth the groundskeeper would be doing up there. Life is full of surprises.

## JAKE

I can't believe it. Elias Greer isn't really the groundskeeper at all. His name is Niles Thomas, and he's the manager for One A-Chord! When Mr. Tabb announced that, I had visions of what I almost did to him. It reminded me again of how stupid it is to judge people and how important it is to keep self-control. Even if Mr. Thomas were just the groundskeeper, I still messed up badly by even thinking about getting revenge. No matter what anyone does to me, I need to learn to treat people with respect. All people. All the time.

Mr. Thomas announced that each band's members were judged on the attitude part of the competition during the week. I sank down in my seat. I had blown it before we even played.

## MO

I knew there was something funny about that Elias Greer! Detectives sense these things. When Mr. Greer—I mean Mr. Thomas—started to announce the winners, I was still shocked. I should have known. I had seen pictures of One A-Chord with their manager before. He did a good job of disguising himself to look a little older.

Up on the stage, he started out really friendly, talking about what a nice group of kids we all are, and how he's enjoyed meeting us. Then he asked us to raise our hands if we've had fun at camp this week. He asked us to raise them higher if we want to do it again next year.

Then he started giving out the prizes. He announced third place first. It was the Heavenly Harpers. I was so excited for them. One of them smiled and waved to me when she got her award. Second prize went to the Royal Rhythmics.

I could see Lance and the rest of the Jammers getting ready to go up and accept first prize, but Mr. Thomas didn't announce first place. Instead, he got really serious.

# JAKE

When Mr. Thomas mentioned revenge, I turned red. I knew he was thinking about what I almost did to his flowers. And I was right. He didn't mention my name, but I was still embarrassed. He told about how I tried to make it up to him by helping him in the gardens.

Then he talked about the things that were done to the band music and instruments. He said that was a totally different story. The vandals had not confessed and changed. Instead, they kept pretending that they were innocent and good.

Finally, he announced that he had been talking about members of the two bands that had been considered for first place. He asked us all a question. "Which one would you reward?"

# PJ

It was like a volcanic eruption, the clapping was so loud. We won! Incredible, but we did. We went up to the stage and One A-Chord came out from behind the curtain. They shook our hands. Gave us trophies.

Candace was clapping so hard I thought she'd break her hands. She was smiling and crying. Cool the way God works things out. I think maybe Candace is okay after all.

# MO

I was shaking and sobbing and laughing all at the same time. It was like a dream, especially when Mackenzie Sutton saw me crying and wrapped me in her arms. We laughed and cried together. I pulled a pack of red licorice out of my pocket and gave it to her. We laughed and hugged some more.

While everyone was still clapping, Mr. Thomas whispered in my ear that my plan worked. The damp powdered drink mix that we left on the windowsill stained Lance's hands when he went back to cut Jake's guitar strings. He was caught purple-handed! That's why Mr. Thomas had all the kids raise their hands so high. He wanted to check them for dye.

## IZZY

I called Mom and asked her to make copies of our band music and bring them with her tonight. I'm glad I keep an extra set at home. When Mom and Dad arrived, I ran to meet them. It had been such a long week. I never thought I could miss home so much.

## PJ

Pris came running up to me like she hadn't seen me in a year. It's funny how much you can miss a little sister. I gave her a big hug. Digby was right on her heels, barking, wagging his tail and jumping up on me. Mom told me that Pris really wanted Digby to come, so they went by the clubhouse and picked him up. I'm incredibly glad they did.

## JAKE

Wally came! I sure missed that hound. I introduced him to Ginger, and they went running off together around the soccer field. I started to run with them, but I couldn't keep up.

Grandma and Grandpa thought Wally looked lonely at Potterfield Pond without Digby, so they asked Mr. Potter if they could bring him. I'm so glad our families could come up to hear us play tonight.

## PJ

We had a picnic with our families. Then set up for the outdoor concert with One A-Chord. It was almost perfect. Until we started to play. Suddenly Digby and Wally were up on stage with us, howling and yipping as usual. Grandpa and Izzy's dad finally got them away from the stage and settled down. But I got tired of the jokes afterwards. No. We are not changing the name of our band to the Heavenly Hounds.

After everyone left, we went back to the cabin. Jake was acting funny. Found potted petunias all over my bunk. I thought that was all. Then I got into bed. My pillowcase was filled with popcorn and there were slithery candy worms at my feet. I laughed so hard. Then Lou turned the lights back on, and we all shared the popcorn. We even ate the worms.

## JAKE

PJ really got me this time. He fooled me and the entire camp, but he still won't admit what he did. He did it right after I had thought I pulled the final prank on him.

When Lou turned off the lights, I got into bed and felt something slithering around my sleeping bag. With a yell, I jumped down to the floor. Lou turned on the lights. I unzipped my sleeping bag as fast as I could. There were three frogs, a garter snake, a cricket and a grasshopper. I couldn't stop laughing long enough to explain that I had put all of those things in PJ's pocket at one time or another during the last week. And PJ, the mastermind prankster, pretended to be fast asleep. He really got me good.

## IZZY

I can hardly believe it's Saturday morning. We're about to leave for home. It's funny how things work out. I came to camp a bossy, opinionated person. I thought of myself as a woman of action. No one was going to mess with my friends or me and get away with it.

I'm afraid I'm still bossy and opinionated. But I've learned a lot about how to treat people and how to control myself.

Not only did the Jammers not win, they also have to pay for all the damage they did to everyone's equipment. I feel sorry for them, not because they got caught and will be punished for it, but because they're missing out on the wonderful gifts that God has for them. If they had trusted him, maybe they'd be spending time backstage with One A-Chord instead of being sent home.

## MO

I can't believe I wasted my whole week at camp looking for One A-Chord. They were on vacation in a beautiful natural setting all right. They were on a four-day cruise in Alaska! The joke was on me and Beth. We couldn't stop laughing when we remembered how silly we were. One A-Chord members are regular people like us. I've learned my lesson. I shared the rest of my licorice with One A-Chord and other kids at camp.

I tried one last prank on Jake to make up for all my wasted time. Put a bunch of gross, slimy animals and bugs in his bed. No one said anything. They must have all crawled out before he got into it. Oh well.

## PJ

What a week! Now that I know what camp is like, I'll be ready for next year. I have 365 days to think up new pranks!

## JAKE

Niles Thomas told me why he was so grumpy. I was right about the music. He has perfect pitch and couldn't handle all the wrong notes. His allergies were acting up too, from all the tall grasses and the makeup he wore to disguise himself. He apologized again. We shook hands, and he gave me a bear hug.

The bus ride home was fun, because everyone got along. It was good to be home again. When Grandpa went out to weed, I offered to help. I found out from Niles Thomas (alias Elias Greer) that gardening together gives you good talking time. Grandpa was excited, and we had lots of fun.

I got new strings for my guitar. It's time to start practicing for the Fourth of July. I hope things go off without a hitch, but then the Q-Crew seems to attract trouble. I wonder what mystery we'll have to solve next time. Whatever happens, when it comes time to perform, Wally and Digby are going to be locked up inside!

# Go for the Godprint

### The fruit of the Spirit is love, joy, peace, patience, kindness, goodness, faithfulness, gentleness and self-control (Galatians 5:22-23).

**Self-control:** All week at camp, the Q-Crew learned about the fruit of the Spirit. And their brushes with disaster taught them important lessons about self-control. Sometimes you can do just what you feel like doing. Other times, it's better to count to ten and think twice. When you put on the brakes, God can help you make choices that honor him.

- How did the things that happened at Crestwater Camp help the Q-Crew learn self-control?
- When do you need to put on the brakes and respond with self-control?

# Family FUNStuff

Get List: __ masking tape

Get your whole family together. Use the masking tape to mark off a straight line six to eight feet long. Now challenge everyone to take turns walking the line without losing their balance. The first time will probably be easy. Make it harder each time. For instance, walk backwards without looking at the line. Walk forward or backwards with your eyes closed. Walk while other people try to tickle you. Then talk about:

- What made it hard to hang onto self-control while you were walking?
- What makes it hard to hang onto self-control when you get upset?
- Tell about a time you honored God with your self-control.